AS BLUE AS THE SKY

CINDY NICHOLS

Copyright © 2019 by Cindy Nichols

All rights reserved.

No part of this book may be reproduced in any form or by any electronic or mechanical means, including information storage and retrieval systems, without written permission from the author, except for the use of brief quotations in a book review.

CHAPTER 1

All the dust surrounding her had stuck on the visor of her helmet, it seemed. *What the heck? I was totally prepared for this. This should be my best time ever.* Through burning eyes, she struggled to see, but the white-out of swirling dust and sand had settled right on her.

Her hand tightened on the clutch of her quad, her foot quickly shifting gears as she was forced to slow down a bit. Her knees reacted instinctively to the bumps ahead of her as she couldn't see them. She'd traveled this course many times, most recently a week ago with her support team in tow, preparing to be the first female rider to win the Baja 250 race on her own in the quad class. She'd practiced and prepared for months ... her father and brother helping her as they had since she'd been old enough to reach the throttle of any quad.

Feeling her best time, her qualifying time, slipping through her fingers, sweat began to seep into the crevices of her helmet, unbidden, as she tried to see her way through the dust storm surrounding her.

Just think, Jess. You know this course. The thought looped endlessly as the encroaching darkness over the desert mountains of Baja California added to her inability to see where she was going. She tried to anticipate the course in her mind, with both the recollection of the map and the visual memory she'd created over the many practice runs she'd made in the previous months.

"Support crew, I can't see where I'm going. Dust storm," she shouted into her in-helmet radio. "Anybody there?" she asked as her pulse quickened, her hands tightening on the throttle.

"We're with you, Jess. Just a few kilometers behind. Hang in there," came a disembodied voice over her radio that she recognized as her twin brother, Cade's.

"Cade, I can't see," she said, slowing slightly again, willing the dust to settle around her.

"I know, darlin'. You're in the middle of a dust devil. A big one. We can see it from here," he said, the cool familiarity of his voice calming her like rain although he was miles away. "Slow down. We'll be there."

She took a quick swipe at her dust-covered visor with her elbow, only managing to create a bigger streak of what was now mud, the dust mixing with the sweat from her lightweight race shirt. The shirt was her favorite, the one with all of the patches from her sponsors that she'd spent years collecting donations from, and she'd always thought it would be her good luck charm. Not so much, she thought. This can't be happening.

"Not now," she muttered, returning her hands to their proper positions on the handles of the quad as the screaming of her engine drowned out any other desert sound. "I can't slow down. My time isn't good enough." Choking on the dust now inside her helmet, her coughs drowned out any reply.

The radio crackled with Cade's voice and her father shouting behind him. She couldn't make out the words, and as she tried to intuitively find the course, the bumps she couldn't see sent the quad airborne, the tires spinning as it rolled and flipped.

This can't be happening, reverberated through her head as she fought against the inevitable. She remembered her father's face as he watched her, so proud, at the starting line. Her own chest had swelled with pride as she saw Cade behind her dad, with his own stopwatch in hand, a wide grin turned in her direction as she donned her helmet.

Her hope of a record-breaking time vanished, and the last thing she felt was her body flying through the air, in what seemed like slow motion, and the sound of the quad thudding on the ground before her. *Just let go*, was the last thought she had, surprising her before she hit the ground, darkness enveloping her as she lost consciousness.

THE CALL HAD COME over the radio throughout the south campos, the string of small beach communities that dotted the coastline of the Sea of Cortez, south of San Felipe. "Medical emergency, 250 course, kilometer forty-two." Colin and James had been the first to respond to the volunteer firefighters' station, and they'd had plenty of practice, both of them ridding the community of an arsonist not long ago, and they quickly donned their gear as the EMT supplies were transferred to the small off-road vehicle they'd need to get to the injured racer.

"Confirm ambulance has been dispatched, anybody?" the captain said as he strode on the scene.

James threw the last of the medical supplies in the jeep. "On their way, Captain. We'll radio with an exact location as soon as we know it." He quickly grabbed the GPS locator, hoping that the coordinates they'd been given were correct. With darkness falling, a moment of worry fluttered through him that they might not be able to find the scene of the accident.

"IT'S A WOMAN," filtered through her mental fog faintly, as her eyes fluttered. "Don't move, ma'am," she heard, wondering if her mind was playing tricks on her as she thought the accent sounded foreign. If anything, she'd expected a Mexican accent here in Baja California. But British?

"Just stay still," she was cautioned once again. It wasn't like she had a choice, as pain shot up from her wrist, sending what felt like lightning bolts directly to her spine. She inhaled deeply, the pain rushing through her again as she realized that she still had her helmet on and it was full of dust. Slowly, she recalled what had happened and her heart began to pound.

"I'm going to take your helmet off slowly, ma'am," she heard, as she felt fingers gently unbuckling the straps beneath her chin.

The wind circled about her forehead as the helmet was lifted off, a hand cradling her head and laying it gently on the dirt she rested on. She felt it cool her as the sweat matting her brown, curly hair began to dry. Of all days not to put it up in a pony-tail. She usually did, but today she'd been too excited, hoping for her best time on the course and she'd forgotten.

The two men she saw when she finally opened her eyes were working quickly around her. Vital signs were checked, and as she tried to cooperate, the dust that had settled into her lungs could no longer be ignored. Coughing in spasms, she felt tears prick her eyes as she saw stars from the pain.

"Ambulance ETA is about ten minutes," he said as he hurried back to the injured woman. She heard them both laugh as he shot over his shoulder, "I think Kyle's on call at the clinic tonight. He should have a fun time with this one."

She ignored them as thoughts of the race flooded her mind once again. Stay still? Her plan was to get back on the bike as quickly as she could and get back on the course. She sat up, willing her legs to move, and was completely surprised when they didn't. She sat, staring, her gaze moving from one of the firefighters to the other. They both were in full firefighter gear, and had brought medical supply boxes that now sat next to her.

"What's your name, darlin'? Can you tell me?"

"Jess. Jess McNally," she said as she again attempted to move her legs. She smiled as she managed to get one of her heels to slide toward her, her knee bending the way it should. "I'm on a pre-run for the 250, and I need to get back on my quad."

"Whoa, there, missie," the tall one said as he turned his head and tweaked it in the direction of the mountains. "I don't think that's a possibility at the moment, so you just rest and we'll get you taken care of."

She followed his gaze and her heart sank as she saw her quad, upside down, among a group of cholla cactus, the most wicked ones there were here in the desert. Once the needle-like spines got in, it was almost impossible to get them out. And last time she'd fallen in one, it had taken hours to get them all out. She wiped the sweat off her forehead, happy she wouldn't be reliving that event. Not today, anyway.

"My father will be here in a minute. Doug McNally. You know, McNally Tires? He'll tell you," she said, content to wait for back-up to get these two set straight.

"I don't know him. Not much of a race fan myself, miss. To be honest, I don't care if you're the Queen of England. We aren't going to let you go anywhere until the ambulance arrives."

"I just have to finish this race. It means a lot to me," she said quietly as she gingerly took off her gloves and set them beside her in the dirt. The pain in her right wrist was getting worse, not better, and she made a concerted effort not to show it on her face. She shook her head, running her good hand through her matted hair and wiping her face with the bottom of her racing jersey. Its blue, black and white colors that she'd been so proud of this morning had all been covered with dust, and it was now a uniform gray color.

She plopped back, lying in the dirt and throwing her arm over her eyes. She tried to wiggle her left leg, hoping that it had just taken a moment for her body to settle and all would be fine now. As she tried to rotate her ankle, she gasped.

Her eyes still closed, she sensed one of the firefighters down by her feet. "Hurts, does it?" he asked quietly as she felt his hands gently on her leg.

"Yes, badly. Can you just tape my wrist so I can get out of here?" she asked, fighting back tears of frustration at her predicament. What would she say to her father? And where was everybody, anyway? All she could focus on was getting up, getting out of there and getting on with her race.

"Sorry, love, I don't think taping's going to be enough to get you out of this fix," she heard, and she sat bolt upright, panic rising in her belly. Finding only sympathy as she searched the firefighter's face, a heavy sigh escaped her. She tried once more to wiggle her fingers, and was horrified to realize he was right as bolts of pain shot up her arm once more.

CHAPTER 2

Cade McNally's head and heart pounded as he gripped the steering wheel of the chase truck, his knuckles white against the black leather that his fingers surrounded. They'd jumped in the truck as soon as they'd lost contact with Jess, riding mostly silently as his father barked directions to him while they followed her GPS signal. They'd been following behind her as she headed toward their other crew members, several miles further up the course. *Why did we space ourselves so far apart?* he chastised himself as worry enveloped him. The sweat on his hands and the blowing sand and dust made it difficult for him to go too fast. Visibility was not good, and his heart beat faster as he wondered what they would find.

He'd immediately called out to the bomberos, the volunteer firefighters here in this community, who were much closer to where Jess had been when they'd last had contact. Trying to hold his voice steady, he had delivered the coordinates and what little information he had. He silently hoped that they were already there. He tried not to think about the fact that the ambulance wouldn't have arrived yet as it would be coming from behind them, all the way from the closest little fishing village of San Felipe, on the Sea of Cortez, where the race course originated.

"Faster, Cade," he heard his father say. He glanced quickly at him in the passenger seat, and saw the concern etched in his face. A man of few words, he knew his father was as worried as he was as he noted his furrowed brow, his eyes intently on the road ahead.

"I can't, Dad. Too much dust."

"Forget the dust, son. It's your sister," his father said quietly. He knew exactly who she was — Jess was his twin sister and the only woman in the family and on the race team, and she held a special place in the hearts of them all, more so since their mother had passed away several years ago.

He cleared his throat and narrowed his eyes, trying to see through the encroaching darkness and all the dust the howling winds had swept up over the course of the day. "Of all days to be so windy."

"You can do it, son. Only another mile," his father said, not taking his eyes away from the road ahead.

His father continued to provide directions, and Cade focused intently on the roads his father was indicating. A mile over these back roads could take a long while to cover, especially with such limited visibility. "Jeez, she shouldn't have been going so fast with this dust and wind," Cade said, realizing too late that it should have stayed inside his head.

"What did you say?" He didn't look at his father, but felt his gaze boring into him as he slowly turned to look at his son.

"Um, nothing. Just thinking out loud."

"Well, don't, if that's the kind of thoughts you have. You know your sister has a goal, and you also know her well enough to know that nothing's going to stop her. She is a McNally, you know."

Cade exhaled, grateful that his father's worry over Jessica had made it a relatively short lecture on the goals and responsibilities of the McNallys, a lecture he'd heard what seemed like about a million times in his short time on the planet.

"Yes, sir," was what he actually said out loud as he cautioned himself to keep his mouth shut, focusing his attention again on the road.

A GROAN ESCAPED Jess's lips as she heard another car approaching and tried to sit up, hoping it was her father and brother, Cade.

The firefighters had set up a big spotlight on a stand as it was getting darker by the minute, and by the light of it she could make out the dark blue support truck with the letters "McNally Racing" on the side. She breathed a sigh of relief as the truck slid to a stop next to the rescue jeep.

Her father jumped out even before the truck had come to a full stop and a lump formed in her throat as she hugged him with her good arm. "I'm sorry, Dad," she said, knowing that her tears needed to be fought back, now. No time for that nonsense.

"Are you all right, sweetheart? We came as fast as we could. What happened?" The words rushed out quickly as her father held her in his strong arms, his tall frame crouched next to her on the desert floor. A sense of safety and familiarity washed over her with the familiar scent of her father.

"I really am sorry," she repeated. "I couldn't see with all the dust. I thought I knew where I was going, but it was my best course time ever, and I didn't want to slow down. Something threw me and I ended up here. And the quad ended up over there." She nodded her head over toward the quad, which still rested upside down.

"That's my girl. You're a McNally, and I would expect nothing less."

Jess heard someone clearing their throat, and looked up to see one of the firefighters, looking down at both of them. "That's lovely, but she could have been killed," he said, his eyebrows furrowed and his lips set in a thin line. "You know that, don't you?"

She watched as her father slowly stood to his full height equal to the firefighter, even with the firefighter's 6' 2" frame, as they stood on opposite sides of her. "And you are..." he asked as his eyes narrowed.

"Name's Colin. Just a bombero, sir, trying to save lives. We see it happen all the time out here. We just clean up the mess." The man's eyes never left her father's, and she noticed the other firefighter come up behind him, standing at his shoulder, as Cade calmly took in the scene from near the truck, before turning to walk away toward the desert. She knew her twin brother well, and so knew that he wasn't about to get involved in anything like this. He'd backed her and her father up more times than she could count. But now, he leaned against the truck, his arms folded, appearing content to know that she was relatively okay and his dad would handle things in his own way.

She breathed a sigh of relief as the sound of the ambulance's siren pierced the air and all three men turned toward it as the headlights and flashing red light stopped on the paved road.

"Do we need an ambulance?" her father asked, peering through the blowing dust toward the flashing red lights.

"She can't move her right wrist without gasping, so I think so," the other firefighter said as he turned back toward Jess. She thought she detected a British accent but couldn't be sure due to the pain. "Colin, I'll take the jeep and run the EMT's in. The ambulance won't make it out here without four-wheel drive."

"Right, mate. I'll be here," Colin replied.

CHAPTER 3

Kyle Morgan set the prescription pad back down on the desk in the examination room as Mrs. Garcia shut the door behind her. When he'd first started volunteering as an intern with Dr. Gomez in San Felipe a few years ago, he'd been flustered by the outpouring of gratitude from the patients who came in, usually with simple ailments with relatively simple fixes. It had taken a while to get used to but now, he realized that this, working with kind and grateful patients, was what he'd always wanted.

When he'd started med school, he'd dreamed about having a small practice like this, with regular people, but had never dreamed he'd be able to do it in Mexico, especially in the place he loved most. Now, that his residency was over, he was still on cloud nine, having accepted Cassie's, offer to be the doctor in residence at the international resort she was building with her new husband. It was coming along nicely, and after this week was over at Dr. Gomez's, he'd be moving to the resort to start his new life.

His attention turned once more back to his patient, and he smiled as he graciously accepted Mrs. Garcia's offering of empanadas, a special type of turnover filled with meat and potatoes, or sometimes fruit, and the hug that followed. "Muchas gracias, Senora Garcia," he'd said, adding, "Buena suerte," wishing her good luck as she took the prescription with her for the antibiotics that would help with five-year-old Raul's ear infection.

All through medical school, he had come down to volunteer at the clinic every chance he got. He'd grown up spending his vacations at his family house in Playa Luna, on the beach of the Sea of Cortez, and he'd met Dr. Gomez as a young boy.

He thought back to the first time they'd met – the first time he'd been stung by a sting-ray and had an allergic reaction – and his mother, Felicia, had rushed him to the doctor. At that time, the doctor had run a very small clinic right near Playa Luna, and over the years, he'd patched Kyle up more than once. Now, as Dr. Gomez wound down toward retirement, Kyle was happy to give him a break so that he could take a vacation of his own. So, he coupled his vacations with volunteering at the clinic. Besides, when he'd decided to become a doctor, it was with the clear knowledge that he would never be one of the doctors who worked ninety hours a week in some hospital. He wanted to help people, yes, but wanted to have a life, too. And that would include as much fishing as possible.

With Dr. Gomez and his family vacationing in Mexico City, Kyle was in charge of the clinic. It was a responsibility he took very seriously. His ears perked and his gut clenched as he heard the ambulance siren approaching.

"What's up, Magdalena?" He asked as he opened the door and walked toward the receptionist's desk. He remembered the days when the doctor's receptionist spoke only Spanish, and although his own Spanish was fluent, he was grateful that Magdalena could communicate with patients, also, in both languages. She would have heard the call on the radio come in while he'd been with Mrs. Garcia.

"Racing accident, doctor," she replied, pointing to the wall that held the poster for this year's Baja 250, its colorful graphics advertising the annual race that was San Felipe's largest event of the year.

He groaned as he placed his elbows on the counter and let his face fall in his hands. He sighed, shaking his head in mock horror, and said to Magdalena, "Oh, yeah. That time again already?"

She smiled at him, shaking her finger, as she said, "Yes, it is. You don't think Dr. Gomez didn't know that when he planned his vacation?"

Kyle's eyebrows shot up as he looked at her. "You've

got to be kidding. With all these crazy racers and copious amounts of beer, not to mention the Tecaté girls, we'll need both of us to patch these folks up. You know how much I hate the races."

"We can hope for a quiet year, Dr. Morgan. But for now, it's an injury from a tumble off a quad. Stable, but in pain and badly injured."

"Who'd be racing in this wind anyway? You can barely see your hand in front of your face with all the dust."

Magdalena shook her head. "You know how they are. They are not to be deterred."

"They're all crazy, if you ask me," he said as he turned to get the examining room ready for his next patient. As he sat, waiting, he thought back to his own riding days, before the accident. He could certainly understand the thrill of riding, covering miles of desert road, inhaling the desert smells of sage and the salt spray of the sea. He'd grown up doing it himself. But those days were over for him, and his memories quickly receded as he saw the approaching red lights of the ambulance.

"The patient's here, Doctor," Magdalena said as she opened the door to the examining room.

Opening the door wider, she ushered in the paramedics pushing the gurney through the wide door. As the ambulance drivers placed the gurney in the center of the room, locking the wheels in place, Kyle saw the familiar bomberos standing in the hallway.

"Colin, James, how are you?" Kyle asked, extending his hand for a hearty shake from both of his friends. Neighbors in the south campos, he'd grown close to James when they'd chased down the fish smuggling ring a while back, and knew Colin from the arsons down south. "Never a dull moment around you two," he said as he gave James a wink.

"No, that's true," James replied, the twinkle in his eye apparent. "This one's interesting. Left ankle...right wrist...not quite sure how bad it is, but I'm sure you can fix her right up, which is what she wants."

Kyle's breath caught in his throat. "Her?" he said, his eyes a little wider.

"Yes, her, and a handful at that," James replied.

"What's taking you so long?" a female voice said from the examining room. "I have to get out of here."

Kyle turned to James with a cocked eyebrow and a quizzical look. "I think I see what you mean. Not the most patient of...patients."

James punched his friend in the arm and motioned for Colin to follow him back out to the jeep. Over his shoulder, he said to Kyle, "Good luck with that one, mate. Her father should be here soon. We'll leave you to it."

Colin coughed into his hand to cover the smile at

James's comment. "Yep, good luck." They both chuckled and headed out with a wave to Magdalena.

Jessica shielded her eyes from the bright light in the examining room, again with her good arm over her eyes. The ride from the accident scene had been a bit bumpy, and she'd fought back tears as the pain continued to send spikes from her wrist, mostly, every time she moved. She still hadn't completely tried to test it, hoping that if she didn't it would be a temporary thing rather than permanent. If that doctor would get in here and tape her up, maybe she'd be able to ride first thing in the morning and still make her best qualifying time.

CHAPTER 4

"Jess, is it? Hi, I'm Dr. Morgan," she heard as the door to the examining room opened and then closed softly. The unmistakable examining room smells of iodine and rubbing alcohol wafted toward her as she felt the doctor by her side.

"Yes, my name's Jess. Something happened to my wrist when I fell and I need your help," she said without lifting her arm from her face. Flat on her back, the pain wasn't so bad, and she hoped this would be quick.

"Well, I can tell you one thing," said the deep, soothing voice that she imagined was cloaked in a white doctor's coat. "It's a good thing that there's no blood or skin puncture. That's a hopeful sign. But I won't know much until we take an x-ray."

She felt his hands gently cut away her riding jersey

from the elbow down—her riding gloves had already been taken off at the scene. A slight groan escaped her lips as he gently touched the outside of her wrist, and as he placed a tiny bit of pressure on it, she gasped, her arm flying off her face as she tried to sit up.

The light in the examining room blinded her momentarily as her eyes adjusted to the light. Finding her balance and sitting up, her eyes widened at the sight of the young doctor standing at her foot.

"Um, you're not Mexican," she said, surprised as her eyes focused on the sights around her.

He turned to her, his smile lighting up his face and she noticed his kind eyes were an unusual green color...almost the color of the sea in the morning. His sandy blond, short hair made his skin look tanned against the color of his eyes. He seemed to be trying to suppress a smile, but not having much luck. "No, I'm not Mexican, but I speak Spanish and I live here as much as I can. But I am a doctor, and I'm here to help you."

She shivered as his hand ran up and down the outside of her calf, surprised at the coolness of the sensation. She'd been hot and sweaty until now, and this, although it felt good, was not something she was used to. Growing up in a house with just her brother for company, she wasn't used to being comforted like this.

"Ouch," she said, wincing as he circled his hand around her ankle.

The doctor stood, removing his hand quickly. "I was just seeing what I could feel from the outside. That's my job," he said, the corners of his mouth turning up into a smile. "From what I can see from the outside, everything looks pretty good," he said with a quick flash of a grin in her direction before he walked to the supply cabinet.

Squirming, she felt the urge to again be off the table and out the door. "You don't look old enough to be a doctor. Where's Dr. Gomez?" she asked, wondering if she was in good hands. She felt a little flustered and wasn't quite sure why. She was always in control, and this time should be no different. Everything depended on this, and she wanted the best care she could find—the sooner to win the race.

"He's on vacation, and I assure you, I am a doctor. A new one, granted, but I've been volunteering at the clinic here for several years. I've seen a race injury or two, believe me." His eyebrows furrowed for a moment, and she thought she noticed the beginning of a frown. Quickly, he turned from her toward the door, and reached out for the wheelchair that had sat ready. Pulling it over to the side of the examining table, he reached out his hand for her to sit up.

"Sorry. I didn't mean to insult you before. It's just that...well, I spend most of my time racing. I'm not used to...needing help. It's not something that goes over well in my world." She hesitated for a moment, not sure that she could or should stand on her injured foot, even though it was feeling a little better. She held her knee out as a test, and winced as she tried to wiggle her toes again. "I don't think I can stand on it. Are we just going to get an x-ray?"

"Yes. Please don't do that until we can assess how bad it is," he said, placing his hand on her knee and gently encouraging her to be still. "I hadn't intended for you to stand. Just slide your legs over to the side of the table here," he said, carefully helping her move to the side and bend her legs.

"I really don't think I can—"

With one swift movement, he picked her up as if she were light as a feather and placed her gently in the wheelchair. She heard a little squeak escape her lips at the surprise, and her eyes narrowed as she looked up at him from the wheelchair. She had never been comfortable not being able to take care of herself, and her pride bristled a bit at being dependent in any way at all.

"Just faster that way," he said as he turned the wheelchair toward the door. "Magdalena will do the x-rays for us, and I'll see you back here in a minute."

As the wheelchair moved out the door with Magdalena behind it, Jess turned to look back into the examining room. It moved out of her view moments later, but she had a split second to see the doctor drop his head in his hands, his shoulders slumped and a weary look in his eyes.

"Is he okay?" Jessica said, wondering out loud what could be wrong with the doctor.

Magdalena sighed as she turned to look at Kyle. "I think he will be, eventually. He's had some racing accidents in his family and he has a little trouble patching people up from the same kinds of accidents."

She turned away, looking toward the x-ray machine, her hopes again raised at the prospect of getting out of there in the near future. "Will this take long?" she said to the woman with long dark hair pushing the wheelchair.

"No, señorita," Magdalena said, smiling to herself as the wheelchair moved down the hallway. "I'll be as quick as I can."

CHAPTER 5

Kyle flipped the light switch on the x-ray viewer and peered at the films in front of him. As they glowed, he viewed Jess's ankle from every angle he could, tilting his head in thought, his mind jumbled as to what to tell her—or, more accurately how to tell her. From what he'd seen of her so far, her determination to get back on the bike, she wasn't going to welcome this news.

As he rolled around his options in his mind, he heard shouting from the reception area. A loud male and Magdalena had gotten into a heated argument. That wasn't like Magdalena, and he frowned as he headed toward the commotion.

At just under 6' 2", he was able to make it to the ruckus quickly. He rushed to the door, throwing it open and reaching the reception area in three long strides. Standing behind Magdalena, he put a reassuring hand on her shoulder. She glanced up at him, her eyes grateful.

"What seems to be the problem here?" Kyle said, his eyes narrowing at the two men before him. The older one, red-faced, opened his mouth as if ready to continue whatever tirade he'd started on. The younger one, with brown hair and streaks of dirt across his face, very much resembled the girl he'd just met, Jess, and stood looking sheepish beside the older man Kyle now guessed to be Jess's father.

"I demand to see the doctor," the older man said, pounding a fist on the counter.

Magdalena continued to try to calm him down, something she was usually expert at. This time, however, her magic wasn't quite working. "Sir, please. I've told you that we are in the process of examining your daughter."

"It's all right, Magdalena. I've got it." Stepping around the corner to where the men were standing, Kyle took a quick appraisal before he spoke. "Mr. McNally, I presume?" he said, his smile wide as he thrust his hand forward. "I'm Dr. Morgan, and am treating your daughter."

The older man's eyes narrowed and he sniffed loudly before saying, "You're not old enough to be a doctor."

He made no move to shake Kyle's hand, and Kyle's eyes grew wider as the younger man, who looked almost identical to his patient, grabbed his hand from beside him, shaking it strongly and firmly. "I'm Cade, Jessica's brother. We're very happy that you're here to help."

Mr. McNally's glare darkened as Kyle said, "Dr. Gomez is on vacation and I'm filling in. We've taken Jess's x-rays already, and her pain is diminishing with some meds we were able to give her. I was just going to bring her into the office to talk about the x-ray results." He made a conscious effort to look Mr. McNally directly in the eye, although he wasn't too pleased with his reception. No wonder Jess was so determined—seemed to be just like her dad. He was pretty sure that his next statement wasn't going to go over too well.

Taking a deep breath, he said, "I'll be with Jess in my office for a bit, and she'll be out when we're done."

Her father's face reddened even more, and his fists clenched at his sides. Kyle looked at Cade, whose widened eyes looked from one man to the other. Straightening up to his full height, he moved toward his father and said, "That's fine, Dr. Morgan. We'll wait here."

"Like hell we will," Mr. McNally said, taking a step toward the door into the back offices. "You have no idea how important this is, son. I'm sorry she's injured, but we need to get her back on that quad as soon as possible. She's been gearing up for this for a long time."

Kyle held up his hands in front of him as he glanced at Cade for support. Cade reached an arm out for his father, pulling him back a step, as Kyle said, "Your daughter is an adult. More than an adult, if I read her chart right. If she gives her permission for you to be in the room, I'll let you know." He returned through the door he'd come out of, closing it behind him. He glanced at Magdalena, and she cocked a brow, nodding her chin toward his office.

"She's in there waiting for you. Let me know what you want to do," she said, straightening her shoulders and turning back toward the reception room.

"I don't know what I'd do without you," he said with a wink as he opened the door to his office.

"Don't you care about your sister?" Cade heard his father say as he sat down, his hands working over the brim of his hat he'd been carrying. It was still covered in dirt, and he looked down at it, unsure of what would satisfy his father at this point.

"Come on, Dad, sit down. She is an adult and he said she's okay, not in pain. It's just routine now, and I'm sure we'll know shortly what's up."

He stood again as the receptionist's phone rang. He watched her look up at his father and then to him as she nodded into the phone, replacing it slowly into its cradle. His breath stopped for a moment, a sense of dread in his chest as she smiled, with an effort at kindness, it seemed to him, and said, "Miss McNally would prefer that you wait here."

The look of surprise on his father's face was one he'd rarely seen. It was more like shock, he thought, as he waited for his father to speak. After a few moments, he gripped his hat tightly, and said, "You okay?" He turned to his dad and watched the color drain from his face as he thudded into a chair next to him.

"What's happened to my daughter?" he said. "The Jess I know wouldn't do that."

"Yes, she would, Dad. You just haven't been paying attention," he said quietly, not sure that his father had heard him.

CHAPTER 6

Jess's hand gripped the cold, steel sides of the wheelchair as she waited for the doctor to hang up the phone. He'd asked her when he came in if she wanted her father in the room. For one swift second she was confused, hadn't really known that was an option. She still wasn't quite sure why she'd told him no. She'd heard them arguing in the reception room, but that was nothing new to her. She loved her father very much but had no illusions as to what others thought of him. Since her mother had died, he'd been a bit more abrasive and loud, but she knew why, so she tried to ignore it. She still wasn't quite sure why she'd replied to the doctor's question with a quick, "No." She hadn't even hesitated; she wanted to face this on her own.

The meds had taken the edge off the pain, although she'd almost fainted when she had to move her arm around for the x-ray. Feeling a little better now, her breathing settled into a steady rhythm as she glanced at the x-rays on the lighted glass behind the doctor's desk.

She tried to remember how many times she'd been in this position before, looking at her bones, broken or otherwise, in black and white in doctor's offices. She peered at them as intently as she could from the opposite side of the large oak desk that stood between her and the backlit representations of her injury on the other side.

"I imagine you've been in this position once or twice before," the doctor finally said from behind the desk.

"What?" Her head jerked away from the films and toward him. "Yeah, once or twice." She winced at the memory of her multiple broken bones, sprains and contusions that she'd met with during her racing career.

He met her gaze, holding it for a moment with one eyebrow cocked. "Okay. I have both good news and bad news. Which do you want first?"

She hadn't realized she was holding her breath until it came out with a whoosh as she said, "Good news. I need some good news." She held his gaze and smiled.

"The ankle's the good news. No broken bones or even hairline fractures. I can see it's been broken before, but it's healed solidly. You were lucky. It should be sore for a while but fine," he said, running his finger over the x-ray of her ankle. He moved to the left, and looked from the x-ray to her, his eyes steady on her. "Moving on to the bad news, can you tell me why this particular wrist looks like it's been in this position more than once...or maybe way more than once." He laid the pointer he had held in his hand down slowly on the desk. The clacking noise it made sounded particularly loud to her for such a small object, and she could hear the clock ticking next to it.

Her good hand instinctively flew to her wrist, cradling it gently even though the pain had subsided a bit with the medication. "Well, this wrist's been a problem. I've broken it a couple of times," she said, looking down from his gaze. It had never bothered her before. She'd fallen, been patched up and raced again. The most annoying part of it had been the time she had to wait to get back on the bike, but her father had helped sturdy it up and she'd never had to wait as long as the doctors said she should. It wouldn't be the first time she'd practiced or raced with a cast on, if it came to that.

He continued staring at her as she spoke. He didn't break his gaze even now. "I see that," he finally said after what seemed like an eternity. "Anybody could see that."

Something in the way he said it made her face flush, and she felt hot under his gaze. "They were all accidents," she said, the defensive tone in her voice not escaping her notice.

The heat continued to rise in her cheeks as she felt

his gaze, still steady on her. She realized that she was biting her lip and abruptly looked up at him, surprised once more by the intensity of his gaze...and her reaction. She hadn't noticed before, but he wasn't much older than she was. Why did she feel like a child? Clearing her throat and gripping the side of the wheelchair with her good hand, she said, "It was just what had to happen to win."

Kyle felt Magdalena's eyes on him as he walked down the corridor to the back of the clinic, entering one of the empty examination rooms and shutting the door behind him. His rapid breathing and sweat under his collar had surprised him when he'd heard the words from Jess. It was just what had to happen to win, she'd said, and all the old feelings took him over. He'd quickly excused himself, knowing he needed to be alone for a moment.

He'd heard the exact same words five years earlier from his fiancée, the last he'd ever heard her say before she slipped into the coma she'd never come out of. Now, this beautiful young woman in his office, with her liquid dark eyes and curly hair, had the same bravado, the same attitude that Maggy had had. And it had been the death of her.

No time for this now, he thought. Get a grip, Kyle. She's not Maggy.

He threw some water on his face and pinched the bridge of his nose, preparing to continue the conversation with this young woman who had flooded him with memories — good and bad. He missed racing, he missed the thrill, but he would never be able to go back there. He felt his heartbeat slowing, and took a deep breath.

He turned back toward his office and saw Magdalena quietly shutting the door behind her. "Is everything all right, Kyle," she asked, the concern in her eyes comforting him.

"Yes, I'm fine," he reassured her, doing his best to give her a broad smile. "We're almost done here. How are the other 'patients' in the waiting room?"

Magdalena laughed, throwing a look toward the men sitting quietly. "They're fine. Just worried."

Kyle looked at the door of his office, his hand on the door knob. "I can understand why," he said as he opened it and went in.

CHAPTER 7

Just another crazy racer, Kyle thought as he picked up the pointer and looked at the young woman in front of him. Granted, it wasn't often that he worked on or with a female rider...but it sure was often that he worked on racers with injuries galore, sometimes pure accidents, but usually involving some sort of recklessness on the part of the rider. It wasn't something that he found particularly admirable anymore, having seen one too many permanent injuries. And it looked like this might be another one if he didn't explain it correctly. She'd confirmed that she'd been injured many times, but now it was his job to explain the consequences of the decisions she'd made—and would be making.

He sat back in his chair, looking intently at the girl in front of him. She seemed bright enough, and certainly committed to her goal. It really was a shame that she was willing to knock herself around like this, risking everything. She was lovely, and her brown eyes seemed to get to him and hint at something deeper than just a sense of competition, but so far he'd seen nothing but that from her.

His shoulders felt tight as he realized it would be up to him to get her to understand her choices ... and for some reason, he wasn't at all confident that he would succeed.

"Jess," he said as he reached again for the pointer on the desk. "May I call you Jess?" He turned away from the x-rays and saw a brief nod from her on the far side of the desk, her dark curls that framed her face bouncing with her head in agreement.

Making a quick circle around her wrist on the x-rays, he said, "You seem very committed to your racing, and I certainly do understand commitment. The problem, though, is how badly you want to be able to continue to do it."

Her sigh didn't surprise him, and he walked around to the front of the desk, right across from her. As he sat on the corner of the desk, she said, "I've explained that I just need to get out of here and back on the quad. The race is coming up and I've been training for this for...well, for years, really. This is the most important one I've ever done."

Her eyes flashed for a moment as he held his gaze steady and tried to assess how she'd take the news. Deciding to just get it out in the open and see where the conversation went, he said, "This wrist has been injured repeatedly, over a long period of time, with much scar tissue and damage. This current injury is painful, right? I believe I heard you yelp a bit in the x-ray room."

A little color crept over her cheeks, and her chin jutted forward as she said, "Maybe."

He couldn't help but laugh — she reminded him of one of those girls in elementary school who you just knew wanted to race with the boys but were too proud or stubborn to admit it.

She crossed her arms over her chest, still cradling her wrist as dust billowed from the jersey. "I don't think you can understand this, Dr. — Morgan, is it?"

"Yes, Dr. Morgan. Have you let this wrist heal completely between injuries? It looks to me like you've taken some risks that maybe you shouldn't have."

"Dr. Morgan," she said, the words coming slowly from her mouth as her eyebrows furrowed her forehead, "I really don't mean to be rude. Honestly, I don't. But my father takes my career very seriously, and it's not something we would take risks with." Her eyes clouded as she said, "This means a lot to me, and to my family. We all care about each other very much, and I don't want to let everyone down."

He sighed as he realized that nothing was going to make this any easier. Kyle watched the blood drain from her face as he said, "That's good to know. But if you don't give up this race and let that wrist heal, you'll be taking the chance that you might not be able to use it without a brace ever, if you can use it at all, permanently."

JESS TRIED to catch her breath as the doctor stood and looked, eyebrows raised, toward the door. "I'm sorry, Doctor, I tried to stop him," she heard the receptionist say as she grabbed the wheel of the wheelchair with her good hand and tried to turn herself around.

"I'm not staying out there one minute more," her father said loudly as he swept past the nurse and into the doctor's office. As she turned toward the door, her father's panicked face was matched only in worry by the one behind it — her brother, Cade's.

"Guys, guys, everything's fine." She tried to muster a smile after the bombshell she'd just heard, and she felt more than saw the doctor turn to her. She glanced quickly at him, and his mouth was open and his hands upturned at his sides.

"Were we just on different planets a minute ago?" His hands dropped to his hips as he looked from Jess to her father. "I think you'd better tell him the truth."

She pushed up with her good foot when she felt a firm hand push her down in place. With an 'oomph', she plopped back down in the wheelchair. She looked down at her hands in her lap, and said, "You're right. Will you tell him?"

"Mr. McNally," the doctor said, "it appears that she intends not to tell you the gravity of the situation. I realize that she has her heart set on racing the 250, but her injury is bad, and while she won't have a plaster cast, she will need to stay completely away from using her wrist and likely her hand until she heals. If she doesn't, and with the number of previous injuries she's sustained, she's risking a permanent one. One that could leave her with limited use of her hand permanently — or worse."

Her forehead fell into her hand as she realized that whatever amount of control she'd had over her universe was quickly slipping away.

"Jess, is this true?" Cade said, her father silent as he looked from her to the doctor. She couldn't read his face, and the familiar anxiety she'd felt when he was displeased crept into her once more.

"We can check with an American doctor, Cade. He would probably see it differently," she said, half-admitting the truth of the matter.

From behind her, she felt the doctor's laughter almost completely rush through her.

"I am an American doctor. I'm just here on vacation in the south campos. But if you want a second opinion, that's certainly your right. In fact, that's probably a good idea. I can wrap these x-rays up for you to take with you up to the states."

She felt a twinge of regret, wishing she could put the words back in her mouth as he turned toward the x-rays. She had three sets of eyes on her, and the rush of indecision, as well as the heat under her collar, was overwhelming. She realized she'd just insulted his integrity, and he had taken very good care of her, but her dream was crumbling before her, and she could see the disappointment in her father's eyes.

It was Cade who spoke first. "Dad, it sounds like Jess wants to see if she can move forward with the race. We're staying in the south campos, too. Maybe the doctor could check in on her and see how it's going? Maybe see if she's healing faster than planned, or monitor her pre-runs?"

"If she continues practicing, the risk of re-injury, or a more extensive injury, is great. She shouldn't be practicing at all, in my opinion, nor should she compete in the race." He sat behind the desk and folded his arms over his chest. His green eyes had grown dark, and if Jess knew him better, she'd have thought he was angry.

She did know her father well, and anger wasn't what she saw on his face. His eyes were dark, too, and his eyebrows formed a V. In times past, she would have expected he'd explode in anger, but his face softened and his voice was quiet when he spoke.

"Doctor, my children have been race kids since the day they were born. It's in our blood, and my wife was part of it, too, before she passed away. You'll have to forgive us for being reluctant to give up on a dream that's been years in the making." His fingers tugged at the brim of the race cap he held in his hands as he continued. "We're staying south also and have a few days, at least, of repair on the quad. Would you be willing to check in on Jess until we see how this is going to go?"

Jess had never seen her father like this — hat in hand, actual worry on his face rather than demand. While it may have been an unusual sight, it didn't change the fact that he'd just asked this young doctor to look after her without consulting her. "Dad, I don't need that," she sputtered. "I'll be fine. I can look after myself."

"I know you can, Jess, but your mom would never forgive me if something big happened to you. It might be time for a little more caution. Just let him help you with some physical therapy while we're working on the quad and we can see how it goes?"

"Ahem," she heard from behind her. She turned to the doctor, his lips turned up into a smile. "Do I have a say in this? I'm down here for the next two weeks and have the time, but I'm not exactly excited by the prospect of looking after an unwilling patient. Or a racer, for that matter. Not my thing."

Jess felt all three sets of eyes turn to her once again and wished the wheelchair would swallow her. She looked at Cade and saw her eyes looking back at her, their connection as twins almost palpable to her now. The pleading in them was more than she could bear.

"If this is the only way I can possibly run the race, I'll do it," she said, looking at her father.

The doctor came around the desk again and stood next to her father. Mr. McNally turned toward the doctor with his own version of pleading in his eyes, one Jess had never seen before. "I'd be grateful for you to look after my little girl, doctor, and see if we could make this work."

Dr. Morgan shook his head vigorously and thrust his thumb at the x-rays. "Those don't lie, sir. I'll tell you right now she should not be running that race, and my opinion won't change. If you still want me to look in on her, I will, but my position won't change."

Jess could actually hear Cade's sigh of relief. She hoped the decision would buy her some time, anyway, and she let out a sigh of her own, hoping nobody in the room heard it.

CHAPTER 8

Kyle had taken extra time splinting Jess's wrist while waiting for the x-rays, so after contact information was exchanged with a time set for meeting the next day, he was able to get them out of the clinic pretty quickly. Magdalena had long since locked up and gone home, so he slipped off his white coat and took out the tape recorder, going over the day's patients for Dr. Gomez's return tomorrow. He wrote his mentor and friend a quick note of thanks for allowing him to help in the clinic and told him he'd be in town in a few days to catch up.

The smell of salt and the sea tickled his nostrils as he walked out of the clinic and to his car. He stopped for a moment and turned out toward the water, watching as pelicans searched for their dinner, a loud growl escaping his stomach as he realized he had missed his. As he turned onto San Felipe's main road and headed toward the oceanfront boardwalk and its enticing array of tacos and other Mexican fare, he was comforted by the sights and sounds of a town he had become intimately familiar with and grown to love. The colorful vendors selling jewelry, blankets and those awesome fish tacos were a welcome sight, and he was surprised by the sense of comfort in his chest.

Turning onto the main drag, the malecón, bordered on one side by the Sea of Cortez and on the other restaurants, vendors and little shops, he pulled his jeep in front of his favorite restaurant and got out. Thinking he'd grab some fish tacos and eat them in the car on the twenty-mile drive to the south campo of Playa Luna that he lived in when he was down, he started toward the door.

Loud voices pierced the air and he turned toward them. Further down the malecón, he spotted a shiny, new truck, big enough to hold several quads. "McNally Racing" was sprawled brightly in blue across the side and was something you couldn't miss with the black background and sponsorship logos covering the rest of it. He considered walking over for a moment, but on hearing Mr. McNally's firm and loud voice, he changed his mind.

"You'll have nothing to do with it, young lady, and that's final," he said, wagging his finger at Jessica as she stood on one foot and leaned against the hood of the truck.

Crossing her arms over her chest, she said, "I am an adult, Dad. You can't tell me what to do."

"I am your main sponsor, and I can pull the plug any time I want to. You're not fixing this quad. If you won't listen to me as your father, listen to me as your boss. You're resting up — we're fixing the bike. Period." He turned from her and walked into the restaurant.

Kyle sighed and shook his head. He realized she hadn't heard a word he said as he headed into his favorite fish taco place, hoping to be on the road before they noticed he was there. He'd had enough for one night.

CHAPTER 9

The wind buzzed through her helmet as she flew through the air again, wishing she could do anything other than wait for the pain she knew would follow. She saw the ground approaching, the four-wheeler spinning out of control, and squeezed her eyes shut, bracing for the coming collision, her arm crunching underneath her on the dirt.

This time, she felt herself caught by strong arms accompanied by a warm and musky scent, feeling safe. This time, warm wafts of sage filtered into her consciousness and she breathed in deeply. This time, she heard herself sigh as she looked up into deep, green eyes, seeing their concern as she fell to safety in his arms...

She awoke with a start, the dream still vivid as she squinted, one eye slightly open. She winced in pain as she tried to move her arm, slowly becoming aware that it was still in a brace. The prickles all the way to her shoulder let her know it had fallen asleep in whatever position it had been in, and she wiggled her fingers to hasten the process of removing the numbness.

She was no stranger to the pain of racing injuries, but never, even in her dreams, had she re-enacted a fall with a different outcome. She felt her face flush as she remembered the ending to this one. How the heck did that darn doctor get in it? He hadn't been helpful at all, even though exceptionally handsome. She shook it off — he had no business in her life or her dreams, and she was in a hurry to get the quad back on the road — with her on it.

Her muscles screamed as she whipped the covers away with her good hand and swung her legs over to the side of the bed. She breathed in deeply, vaguely noticing the smell of the salty air and realized she was in the casita they always rented right on the water of the Sea of Cortez. The house was formed around a huge, circular room made of the ladrillo brick that was a dark red, creating a coolness against the hot desert sun.

Gingerly standing to make sure her legs would hold her, she opened the window that looked east over the white sand and to the crystalline blue waves that lapped against the shore quietly. Nice, she thought, but not on my agenda today. She turned away just as a flock of pelicans flew by, their search for daily fish starting early.

She grabbed the bottle with the pain-killers, shaking out a few, tossing them back with the bottle of water next to her bed, and looked up at the knock on her door.

"Hey, Jess, you up yet?" Cade's voice startled her, and she realized she hadn't gotten dressed.

"Be right there, Cade. I need a quick shower," she said as she grabbed her jeans and riding jersey.

"Breakfast is ready and we need to talk. No time for that. Dad's waiting. Hurry up," he said, his voice trailing off back toward the big kitchen in the center of the house.

"I'm at least going to brush my teeth. Hold on," she shouted at him, moving toward the bathroom they shared in between their rooms. She looked longingly at the big glass block shower, its interior walls covered floor-to-ceiling with inlaid, smooth beach pebbles, thinking how good it would feel to wash all the desert dust from her body. She'd been exhausted when they'd gotten home the night before and had barely been able to splash water on her face before falling into bed.

She'd not been able to do a very good job of it with one hand, and she noticed the streaks of dirt still covering her as she looked in the mirror on the wall, also surrounded by shells. Grabbing a wash cloth, she was able to at least get the final streaks off her face and neck, the cool water waking her up a little more as she wondered what the rush was all about. Teeth brushed and face, at least, streak free, she grabbed at her brown, shoulder-length hair and wondered what she could do with it — one hand being unavailable. She grabbed a pony-tail holder and tried to put it up, but her hand was still tingling, mostly numb, and she gave up the effort to calm her curly locks. She grabbed a white elastic headband and threw it in her hair — at least that would keep it out of her face.

Sitting on the bench outside the glass block shower, she fumbled with her jeans, not quite able to slip them on. She knew she'd have an equally difficult time getting her racing jersey on and grumbled to herself as she grabbed a bright pink skirt she'd brought in case it was really hot, managing to pull on a loose, white tank top before slipping on flip-flops. *My race boots are going to be a bear to get on with one hand*, she thought, hoping that no one at breakfast would notice the difficulty she was having, and it seemed like forever before she got herself put together.

Her stomach grumbled as she opened the door to her bedroom and walked to the kitchen. She'd spent a fair amount of time in Mexico, but the smell of chorizo and eggs always made her famished. The spicy Mexican sausage was one of her favorites, and rolled up in a tortilla with eggs and hot sauce — even better.

She was so hungry she didn't notice two sets of eyes staring at her as she served herself a plate — with her back to her brother and father — furtively using only one hand. As she came around and sat down at the table to eat, the warm tortilla pierced through a bit of the numbness as she picked it up and tried to scoop the chorizo and scrambled egg mixture into it. Her fingers weren't cooperating, though, and she'd only managed to move the eggs around as they skidded from one side to the other before her fork clattered on the ceramic plate and she sighed in disgust.

The same two sets of eyes were still on her as she looked up. "What are you looking at?" she asked, seeing the alarm on the faces staring at her.

Her twin and her father exchanged quick glances before looking down at their own plates and resuming eating. Her father cleared his throat, placed his fork on his empty plate and sat back into his chair.

"We have some things to talk about, young lady," he said as she met her brother's gaze before he quickly looked away, got up and started clearing the table. "What the doctor said last night is not to be taken lightly."

She opened her mouth to protest, but shut it just as quickly as her father held up his hand, palm out, stopping her from voicing any opinion. His face was dark and clouded, and she knew from experience it wouldn't be smart to try to speak until he had said what was on his mind.

"I know you've had your heart set on this race for a long time. We have, too, both your brother and I and the other sponsors. Hell, you were our bright light for this year. However," he continued, "no single race is worth a permanent injury, Jess. Your brother and I have talked, and we think you should just disqualify yourself due to injury and try again next year." He folded his napkin, placed it in his lap and folded his arms across his chest. Not a good sign.

"Dad, I'll be fine." Her heart clenched as she thought of all that training time going to waste, and how disappointed the crew and sponsors would be. "I want to get in the garage and start working on the quad. We only have a week and it needs to be in shape quickly so I can train some more."

"I don't think you're listening to me. I haven't changed my position since last night."

Her frustration formed into tears that threatened to spill — something she refused to do in front of her father. "I can do this. Please."

"Jess, you can't even get eggs off your plate. How are you going to fix a quad, let alone ride one?" he said, his voice rising. His brows were furrowed and his eyes narrowed. "I know you have always gotten your own way, and it's probably my fault. But this is non-negotiable."

"Dad, please. You asked that doctor to come help, see if I could get my arm back in shape to ride. Can we wait and see how it goes?"

"He didn't sound too encouraging about that possibility," he said, leaning forward and clasping his hands in front of him. That was a good sign, Jess knew, so she pressed forward.

"I'll make you a deal. I'll stay out of the garage so

you and the crew can fix the quad if you'll re-evaluate about letting me ride when it's done. It should take a week, right, to get all the parts? We should know by then how my wrist is." Never one for being too girly, she thought this required everything in her arsenal. She smiled her biggest smile and made a face, the one that always made him laugh and had since she was a little girl.

From the kitchen, Cade said, "No fair. That's cheating." She turned just in time to catch the grin he wore before he turned to start putting things back in the refrigerator. He'd always been on her side and seemed to be even now.

Her father let out a sigh with a whoosh, shaking his head as he said, "I don't know why I do this. Okay, deal. You do everything the doctor says, we fix the quad, and we'll decide in a week what to do. Which will be what's best for you, Jessica. Come on, Cade, the guys'll be in the garage by now. Let's get on it."

She watched as the door shut behind them, waiting until it was completely closed to try to rub the numbness out of her hand as she grimaced. She breathed a sigh of relief as she'd won this battle — realizing clearly that she was far from winning the war if her hand didn't cooperate. Still hungry, she grabbed an apple, feeling positive she could eat that with one hand. She turned to the big French doors behind her and looked out to the water as she felt the warm sea breeze on her face.

Great, she thought. An entire week with absolutely nothing to do. She'd never had that much time on her hands and couldn't even imagine how to occupy her days as she was banished from the garage. She tossed the apple core in the trash and decided the best start might be to take a shower. Or to at least try.

CHAPTER 10

One cup of coffee was all he had time for if he wanted to get to Jess's on time. The sun over the water had woken him early — early enough, he thought, for a quick swim in the warm water, so he'd headed down to the beach.

The cool breeze played on his face as he set his to-go coffee cup in the sand, wiggling it down next to his towel so it wouldn't fall over. He stretched his arms to limber up a little bit. Kicking off his flip-flops, he found a little entry to the beach that was all sand and walked toward the water. As he walked, he noticed the small, round jellyfish that had washed up on the shore and avoided them, although he knew he didn't need to. These were beautiful, a deep blue that reminded him of jelly beans, but had no sting to them.

Sighing as he wiggled his toes in the warm sand, he felt the temperature change immediately when he made it to the tide line and onto the hard, wet sand between the lapping waves. The tide range at Playa Luna, the south campo where his family's house was, could be extreme with a full or new moon, one of the most extreme tides in the world. Today, though, the tide was pretty far in — perfect for a swim out and back before breakfast.

He walked into the water, employing the Baja shuffle that had been ingrained in him since he was a kid...shuffling his feet as he walked into the waves, hoping that the sting-rays wouldn't like it and would swim away from him. The water was cool on his legs, and as he got deep enough to swim, he jumped fully in, enjoying the cool sensation on his skin.

As he got in his swimming rhythm, the cool water rushing past him as he swam toward the lighthouse, he found himself turning over the events of the night before in his head.

The girl had been so stubborn and hell-bent on racing. And her father so completely adamant, in the office. He thought how surprised he'd been when her dad had threatened to pull the plug, and hoped maybe he'd have an ally in him.

An ally? What do I care? I don't even know this woman, he thought, his arms spinning rhythmically as he kicked harder against the waves. He did remember thinking that she was striking to look at; not the classic California girl with blue eyes and blonde hair. No, she looked a little more Mediterranean, her dark eyes and curly brown hair looking as if they'd be at home in Tuscany or Brazil. Exotic.

But that fire in her eyes gave him pause. She looked determined to not only ride in this race, but win. And if that was the case, he didn't want to have too much to do with her. It wasn't his race, and it wasn't his problem.

He turned on his back, working his backstroke, and looked at the cliffs of Playa Luna, the houses dotting the top and the waves crashing onto the sand below. The colorful flags flying over the houses always made him chuckle. A certain type of person gravitates to this spot, he thought, chuckling at the banners ranging from butterflies to peace signs to boxer shorts, He shook his head and smiled, realizing that he was one of them now, realizing in an instant that he'd always wanted to be...different. With a life that he could lead more freely without being a slave to credit cards and commutes.

He glanced at his diving watch and realized he was running late. He headed back to shore, dried himself off quickly and headed up to the house.

THE COOL WATER of the shower raining down on Jess's head had helped a little with the fuzziness in her brain. As the dust and dirt slid off her body, she let herself relax and the flood of memories hit her all at once. The first quad she'd ever ridden, when she was still so tiny her feet didn't reach the ground and her father had to put her on and take her off. The exhilarating rush she'd felt the first time she'd won a race. The glow on her mother's face at the finish line. The panic she'd felt when she'd heard of her mother's accident. Her father's stoic insistence that they continue to race — and to win — to make her mother proud. Her own determination to win this particular race.

The doctor had said she was determined. But when he'd said it, she clearly sensed that what he meant by it was not the same as when her father said it to her, over and over. Not a compliment from the doctor, by any means. The flutter of butterflies in her stomach returned with the memory of his sandy hair and green eyes, boring into her as he gave her the bad news about her wrist. She'd been surprised that his touch had made her tingle. She was around men all the time, day in and day out, but hadn't had that experience before. But he clearly didn't understand or respect her choice to continue to race, and since it was non-negotiable in her mind, she dismissed the thought of him. *What do I care what he thinks about me, anyway?*

She shook her head, turning the water off and reaching for her towel. Racing was all she'd ever known, like her parents, and now wasn't the time to second-guess what had been her pleasure and her passion — and her responsibility.

She felt a twinge of pain in her wrist as she dried

off. Her right hand was virtually useless to her, and she gingerly pulled on a sundress, the cool, pale pink cotton brushing lightly against her clean skin. Her lips curved up into a smile as she realized why her brother had made the comment he did about her looking like a girl. Down in Baja was the only place she ever wore a dress, and it had begun only as an effort to stay cool on some of the hotter days. Even by the ocean, it could get hot and humid if there wasn't a breeze — and she was grateful that today, there was a delightful one.

Pulling a quick comb through her hair, she grabbed a pink headband she'd hastily stuffed in her bag. *No wonder Cade didn't recognize me. I barely recognize myself.* With a final glance in the mirror and a quick rub of her wrist, she slid her feet into flip-flops and headed toward the garage.

KYLE HOPPED out of the shower, quickly threw on shorts and t-shirt and grabbed the keys to the yellow Manx, the dune buggy he'd fixed up and given it to his mom for Christmas. The odd little dune buggy still ran, even though that had been more than a decade ago, when he'd still been in high school. Even though it had a roll bar, he'd stopped driving it completely after Maggy died, and it was only recently that he'd been able to get back in it without having to get right back out and into a regular car with a roof.

He'd found the campo that Jessica was staying in on the map hung on the kitchen wall. Just a kilometer south, he glanced at the tide calendar and noticed that it was low tide. He quickly decided to go down to check to the beach to check on her. He'd always taken the beach any chance he had.

The engine turned over on the first try—only after he'd put on his seat belt— and his sense of satisfaction that it still worked perfectly, after all these years, made him smile. He backed out of the garage and turned onto the dirt road, heading through the arroyo separating his campo from the campo south and turned east, onto the sand.

His hair rustling in the wind, he took his sunglasses from his head and placed them firmly over his eyes. Both hands gripped the wheel as he made his way onto the hard-packed sand that had recently been underwater and turned south. He laughed as he spotted fish jumping. He slowed slightly at his favorite fishing spot, wondering if he was passing up a good yellowtail day, then remembered he could always go later.

He turned into the camp Jess's father had mentioned and as he crested the dune, he couldn't miss the truck he'd seen the night before with "McNally Racing" plastered on the side. He'd stopped following the races years ago, after the accident, and had never heard of Jess McNally, or any McNally's, period.

Rolling to a stop next to the garage, he noticed the mechanical crew swarming around what looked like a quad in the center of the garage. The smell of gas and oil hit his nostrils as he hopped out of the car.

Kyle turned the corner of the garage and felt his eyes widen as he took in the sight. At least seven men were standing next to the almost destroyed quad, which was lifted up on a stand. He recognized Cade, Jess's brother, standing closest to Jess, his arms folded over his chest. Jessica stood next to him, and didn't seem too happy about being left out of the repairs, her feet shuffling as if she didn't quite know what to do with herself.

What had really surprised him, though, was the sight of Jessica. The lovely woman in front of him bore no resemblance to the dirt-covered woman with matted hair that he'd met the night before. As she turned to look at him, he did notice one thing that remained the same—her eyes. The dark eyes that had struck him last night as having determination and drive in them were there, but framed by lovely brown curls. Her pink sundress and pink headband almost made him laugh, so different it was from her racing jersey and torn race pants she was wearing when they'd met.

"What are you laughing at?" she asked, and he instantly realized that he had been smiling...a smile which evaporated as all eyes turned toward him.

"I'm not laughing," he said, crossing his arms over his chest, a look of understanding directed at Cade.

"Oh, Doctor, perfect timing." Mr. McNally strode

over to him, offering an outstretched hand. Kyle took his hand and matched his smile. "As you can see, we have our hands full on several fronts," he said, his eyes narrowing as he turned to his daughter.

"I just want to help," she said quietly.

Cade laughed. "You look too much like a girl to help."

"I heard you this morning, Cade. Not funny, for the second time." She looked from face to face, and Kyle was sure she was finding no compassion.

"Seriously, Jess, you're supposed to rest your hand, and we've got it covered." He turned to Kyle, throwing up his hands. "Can you help us out? Get her out of here, maybe?"

"What?" Kyle and Jess said in unison, looking toward each other at the same time.

"That would be perfect," Cade said, grabbing a wrench and heading toward the quad. "We don't have too awful much time to fix this, and she won't leave us alone."

"Oh, Cade, you know I just want to be part of the team." Her eyebrows furrowed as she looked from her father, to her brother and to Kyle. The other crew members had slunk away and started working on the bike.

"Doctor? Some help here?" Mr. McNally said as he ripped his hat from his head, running his hand through his hair.

"Call me Kyle. And, um, I guess I can take her with me up to the new resort. I was headed there next."

"Well, I'd sure appreciate it. I know you'd have your hands full, but I don't need her in here bugging us."

"Bugging you? I'm the best mechanic on the team," she said, without a hint of arrogance. She said it as a simple statement of fact. Based on the lack of objection from the race crew, or her father or brother, Kyle figured it must be true.

"Look, you really do need to go easy on your hand. In fact, you shouldn't use it at all if you want it to heal properly. Seriously, I was headed up to have lunch with my friend, Cassie, at the resort. She's like a sister. Why don't you come with me? Have you seen it?" he asked, noticing the looks of gratitude from both Mr. McNally and Cade.

"Is she that marine biologist who married the guy building the resort?" Jess asked, her shoulders sagging a bit as if accepting defeat.

Kyle smiled and nodded. "I'll tell you the story on the way. I haven't seen her for a while, and I think you'd probably like her."

"Actually, I haven't been up there since they started," she said, sounding a little defeated but willing to take a step back.

Mr. McNally whipped out his wallet from the back pocket of his jeans. He crushed a hundred-dollar bill in Kyle's hand, and with another firm handshake said,

"Great. You kids go have a good time, and we'll be working here when you get back."

Kyle closed his mouth that had fallen open at the quick gesture, and turned to Jess, the corners of her mouth now turning up into a smile.

"He rarely takes no for an answer, so you just saved yourself a lot of time arguing. Trust me," she said, shaking her head slowly.

"Go on, now, get out of here," Mr. McNally said over his shoulder as he headed back toward the quad.

CHAPTER 11

"How's the pain today?" Kyle asked as he led her over to the Manx.

She looked at the yellow Manx, beautifully restored, and didn't even hear his question. "Wow, that's a nice one. And yellow, too. Not many yellow ones anymore."

She saw Kyle's grin and noticed how his eyes lit up as he looked at the dune buggy. "I restored it myself. It was a gift for my mom."

She let out an appreciative whistle as he helped her into the passenger seat. He helped her lower herself into the seat and came around to the passenger side, hopping in as he held onto the roll bar. "Do you need help with your seatbelt?"

Confused for a minute, she realized he was serious. "Seatbelt? Are we going on the road?" She'd assumed they would be driving on the beach, as she'd heard the resort had made it possible to get through the mud flats.

He turned to look at her, his eyes intense. "Yes, we're going on the beach, but no seat belt, no ride."

"You're serious, aren't you?" she asked, wondering if he was the only person in Baja who wore a seatbelt. She didn't remember the last time she'd worn one in a buggy, at least at the beach when she wasn't racing, but his eyes had clouded and she thought it would be better to comply than argue the point. There was something about this guy that she couldn't quite put her finger on. He seemed nice enough, friendly even, but when anything came up about racing or speed, he clammed up and clouded over. Maybe it had something to do with what the nurse had told her.

"Okay, but I don't think I can do it with this brace on. My fingers can barely move." She held up the black brace, barely wiggling one of her fingers. His face changed immediately and he went into doctor mode, taking her wrist gently in his hand and pinching one of her fingers slightly.

"Can you feel that?" he asked, putting a small amount of pressure on her thumbnail.

"Yes, I can." She watched as he looked at her hand intently, turning it over in his hand and repeating the process with each of her fingernails. She saw his jaw clench as he examined her hand, and noticed the light stubble that had appeared on his chin, sparkling a little bit in the light and matching the sandy color of his hair. Although she wished they wouldn't, the butterflies returned and she felt her face flush a bit as his scent wafted over her.

And it flushed a little bit more as he looked up and met her gaze while she'd been staring at him. Her breath hitched and she looked quickly back down at her hand, wishing he hadn't seen her.

"Well, looks like everything's okay for now," he said, setting her hand on her lap and reaching over her for the seatbelt. She held her breath as he clasped her in, hoping this feeling would go away and she could get back to what was most important...the race.

They were quiet on the short trip up the beach after he'd given her a run-down on the resort, both lost in thought. Jess hadn't been to the beach on a trip down in years, and the salty air massaged her senses. The smell was clean and fresh, and the cool wind on her face and flipping through her hair...one of her rare drives without a helmet...felt great for a change.

"Stop," she said as they approached the north point of Bahia Santa Maria.

He glanced at her quickly and slowed the Manx to a stop. "Everything okay?" he asked, concern in his eyes as he looked at her hand.

"Oh, sorry, yes. I just wanted to know what happened here," she said, pointing to a row of three brick houses that appeared to have collapsed onto the beach. She popped the seatbelt open—much easier than closing it, she found—and pulled herself up on the roll-bar with her good hand. She settled on top of the seat she'd been sitting in so she could see better.

Kyle followed her gaze and turned back toward her, slowly shaking his head. "Isn't it awful? The tides have changed here in the last few years, and these houses used to be much further from the high tide. See those retaining walls on the houses at each end? The folks who live here had to build those to stave off damage. This past summer, a hurricane passed through and the combination of the high tides and storm took these out."

She stared at the rubble of these lovely round houses, all built with the beautiful red ladrillo bricks that she thought was so lovely. Her heart tugged at the thought of how devastating such a loss would be, as most people loved this place with a passion. "What will they do?" she asked, as she sat back down in her seat, cursing her decision to wear a dress as she tugged it down beneath her and hoped he was still looking at the houses. She looked up to find him looking right at her, his face covered with a wide grin.

"Need any help?" he said, laughing.

She felt her brow furrow as she squinted at him. "I don't like being laughed at."

"So you've told me. Twice, I think it is. I'm not laughing at you...isn't that how the saying goes?" The twinkle in his eyes made them appear even more deep, and she couldn't stop the smile that curved her lips.

"I guess I do look kind of silly. I'm not used to

wearing dresses," she said, her skirt now firmly back where it needed to be.

"Silly wasn't the word I would have used. I was thinking something more along the lines of...charming," he said as he looked back to the house quickly.

She cleared her throat, wondering if that was the first time any man had classified her as charming, and decided that it in fact was the first time. Charming was not a word that most of the men she hung around with used to describe her.

Still a little flustered, she asked again. "So, what are these people going to do?"

"Can you see the larger structures behind these houses? When the damage started to happen more and more frequently, in little bits and pieces, most people built an additional house directly behind. These lots are all pretty big and they had plenty of room to do it. I don't know many people in this campo, so not sure of the whole story. But it really is a shame."

He started the buggy and headed north, staying mostly on the firm sand. She looked over and noticed that his hands were placed exactly at ten and two on the steering wheel, and he seemed to be paying a great deal of attention to his driving...which was incredibly slow.

"Can't you go any faster?" she asked, raising her eyebrows.

"Um, no. I can't. This is fast as I go in a dune buggy.

It must be excruciating for you as a racer," he said, his voice suddenly flat.

She thought maybe she'd insulted him, but hadn't meant to. "I was just teasing. I'm perfectly happy taking in the scenery."

He turned to look at her quickly before turning back to the road. His quizzical gaze seemed to be assessing whether or not she was making fun of him, and he said, "It's just the way it has to be, Jess. We'll get there."

She looked ahead and noticed the spots of what looked like small casitas growing larger. As they got closer, a larger building came into view past the smaller casitas and a huge area of the sea looked cordoned off, almost like a marina with wooden docks reaching out into the water. "What's that?" she said as they passed the first dock.

"That's Cassie's sanctuary, a breeding place for the vaquita porpoises. Looks like it's turning out nicely."

"That's an amazing story, what she did. I read about it in a magazine. I'm looking forward to meeting her," she said as they circled in on a very big, incredibly lovely brick house that stood on top of a dune. It was surrounded by brightly-colored bougainvillea—red, purple, orange and even white ones. Large trees loomed over a courtyard where a very pretty woman, about her own age, stood with a big smile, waving at Kyle. Her blonde hair blew in the breeze, and as they walked up the stairs, a tall, dark man stepped up from behind her and wrapped his arms around her waist.

As they reached the top, she moved quickly toward Kyle, throwing her arms around his neck as he met her embrace.

"Kyle, it's so good to see you. You haven't been here since the wedding!" she said, standing back with her hands on his shoulders. "You look great."

"Thanks, Cass, so do you," Kyle said as he extended his hand to the tall man. "Hi, Alex. Great to see you. Cassie, Alex, this is Jess McNally. She's a racer."

They both turned to Jess with wide smiles, and Cassie extended her hand. "Oh, I'm sorry," Jess said, holding up her right hand with the brace on it, waving weakly.

"She was in a quad accident last night and turned up at the clinic. I patched her up, but she's got to lay off racing for a while and her father asked me to get her out and about," he said. Jessica was grateful that he hadn't shared the reason her father had wanted her out, and glanced at him gratefully.

He smiled in return, and said, "How's everything going here? Looks like it's changed quite a bit."

"Oh, it sure has. We're making great progress. I'm sure you saw the sanctuary on your way in," Alex said, placing his hand on his wife's shoulder as she turned to him and smiled.

"I can't believe you guys pulled it off," Kyle said, his hand raised over his eyes as he looked out over the sea.

"It's amazing," Cassie said. She grabbed Kyle's hand and pulled him toward the big French doors and into the lovely brick house. "We've got lunch ready for you. Come inside and I'll tell you all about it."

Jessica smiled as Alex offered her his arm and escorted her inside behind the life-long friends who were talking a mile a minute, arm in arm.

CHAPTER 12

As Jessica and Alex walked into the beautiful dining room, he turned to her and held his finger to his lips, his eyes twinkling as he quietly said, "Shhh. It's a surprise."

She couldn't help but laugh at the look of shock on Kyle's face as he stopped dead in his tracks, his eyes wide.

"Surprise," shouted at least thirty people, and Cassie jumped up and down as she clapped her hands together.

Jessica had no idea who most of these people were, but she couldn't help be happy for Kyle...whatever he'd done to deserve the surprise. Was it his birthday, she wondered? She hoped he would have told her that, if it was.

Alex tapped the glass of champagne he was now holding, and cleared his throat, encouraging the crowd to silence. "Thank you all for joining us here. It is a momentous occasion, and we'd like to congratulate Kyle — and us, here at the resort — for his decision to accept our offer of becoming resident doctor for us and our guests. We couldn't have wished for a better physician...or a more honorable man. He will make us proud here, I am positive. Congratulations, Kyle, and thank you," he said, hoisting his glass to a round of applause, whistles and cheers.

Cassie beamed as she rushed to hug her friend, her smile spread ear to ear. "You surprised?" she said, hugging him tightly.

"Um, I don't know what to say, Cass. Thank you." He gave her a peck on the cheek as he turned to hug Alex as well. "I truly am excited, and thanks for having friends and family come to celebrate. Can't believe I get to start in a couple of weeks," he said, glancing around the room.

"The sooner the better," Alex said. "We've got a whole clinic to design and set up before we open, and that day's coming fast."

"I didn't know you were going to work here," Jessica said, her eyebrows raised. "What an exciting thing." She glanced around the beautiful house and out the huge, plate-glass windows to the ocean. In the distance, she could see the beginnings of the resort, a stable, and the smaller casitas they'd passed on their way in.

"Good decision, lad," she heard from behind her,

and she immediately recognized the man who had helped her after her accident.

"Thanks, Colin," Kyle said as he shook his hand. "Nice to see you again, Hanna," he said to the stunning woman next to Colin, her dark braid down her back complimenting her colorful Mexican skirt.

"You too, Kyle. Welcome aboard," she said with a smile as she leaned in and kissed his cheek.

"Here come James and Megan," Kyle said as he waited for another couple to approach, Jessica recognizing the man from the accident also. His white hair and beard didn't fit with his age, as she judged him to be not older than fifty, and the lovely woman on his arm's long, blonde hair and smiling blue eyes made her seem a perfect match for him.

"All of you, I'd like to introduce Jessica McNally," Kyle said.

"Have you forgotten, son," Colin said, poking an elbow in Kyle's arm. "We're the ones who brought her to you." He laughed and winked at James.

"Ah, this is the young racer you told me about, James. You're right, she's lovely," Megan said as she offered her hand to Jessica.

Jessica felt her face flush, her memory instantly returning to the previous night when she'd crashed and flew through the air. "Oh, goodness. It's nice to officially meet all of you and thank you for taking such good care of me last night. Good time to apologize, too, as I was thrown for a loop. Literally. And I don't think I was an easy patient."

Kyle, Colin and James exchanged glances and broke into hearty laughter. "That's an understatement, madam, but apology accepted," James said, squeezing his wife's hand. You back in the saddle again, so to speak?"

It was Kyle and Jessica's turn to exchange glances. She couldn't quite read his face, but thought she saw a flicker of concern.

"Not yet. Doctor's orders...and I'm following them," she said, raising her glass to the group.

"Best thing for you, Jessica. Kyle knows what he's doing," Cassie interjected. "And these guys are great at getting folks to him. Colin here is our fire captain and Hanna is our horse trainer and trail leader."

"I wondered about the red cowboy boots," Jessica said, laughing. "They suit you."

Hanna lifted up her skirt, kicking out the heel of the cowboy boots that had become her trademark after the arsonist had been caught. "Thanks. Now if only I knew how to line dance."

As the people stopping by to congratulate Kyle filled their plates with the colorful array of seafood laid out on a long table by the windows, Jessica listened mostly in silence as the group of friends caught up over an impressive lunch of cold shrimp cocktail, chips and salsa and the most amazing guacamole she'd ever had. She remembered that the shrimp cocktail down in

Mexico was different...not cold steamed shrimp with cocktail sauce like ketchup. This one was authentic and traditional, with shrimp, tomato juice, jalapeños, onions and lime juice, almost more like a ceviche. It was one of her favorites, and she happily dug in while listening to the current progress on the porpoise sanctuary and resort that Cassie and Alex were creating. Margaritas had been offered, but she politely declined, not sure it would interfere with her pain medication and wanting to make sure she was healing as best she could.

After much laughter and great stories, Cassie turned to Jessica and said, "So, you're a racer, Jessica? Here for the 250?"

"Yes, I am. I'm competing in the quad class, and want to be the first woman to win."

Kyle cleared his throat and she turned quickly to look at him. His eyebrows were raised as he looked at her intently.

"Well, I think I'm competing," she said, "but it will depend on how I'm healing. Was that the right answer?"

"Hey, I'm just your doctor, not your manager," he said, turning toward Cassie. "She's got a pretty bad injury which could cause her permanent damage if she injures it again too soon. I've informed her of that, and it is hers to decide what to do. We're kind of waiting for a few days for a re-evaluation, and I'm trying to keep her laying low until then."

Cassie looked at her Kyle, then at Jess, then turned back to Kyle. "That must be challenging for you," she said as she covered Kyle's hand with hers.

Kyle cleared his throat again as a shadow crossed his face. "I'm fine, Cass. Right now, I'm just trying to help keep her busy. Any suggestions?"

Cassie's look of concern for her friend took a moment to fade, and Jess wasn't sure what to say. She hadn't intended to make things difficult for Kyle, and was grateful that he'd accepted her father's request to give her something to do. If it weren't for him, she'd be going stir crazy.

Alex stood, his hand again on his wife's shoulder as he called for dessert. "Do you like to fish, Jess?" he asked as he poured margaritas for the three who were drinking them.

"I do, but I'm not sure how much I could do with one hand." She laughed as she held up her hand with the brace on it, barely able to wiggle her fingers.

"Of course, but it's nice to be out on the water, even if you're just watching someone else fish."

Cassie smiled brightly, adding, "These fishermen are obsessed. Every day is a fishing day. But honestly, that wouldn't be a bad idea. You could head down to Gonzaga Bay and fish there. I think the yellowtail are running, and you could stay at our house down there."

"How long does it take to get there? I really can't be gone too long with the race next weekend," Jess said, stealing a quick look at Kyle. His expression was blank, and he fiddled with the flan that had been placed in front of him. The custard with caramelized sugar on top looked delicious, and it distracted Jess long enough to pick up her spoon and miss the look Kyle shared with Cassie.

Cassie set her dessert aside after finishing half of it, her gaze steady on her lifelong friend. "You could just head down. The road is through now, and it takes a little over an hour to get there. It's a lovely drive, and a beautiful bay. Worth the trip, and it would kill a day, at least. You could spend the night if you wanted to."

Jessica felt the flan stick in her throat and she coughed, dropping her fork and raising her hand to her mouth. "Oh, I think just a day trip would be great. I don't want to trouble Kyle any more than that, and I have to get back on the quad."

She turned to Kyle, her eyebrows raised, wondering what he was thinking. He looked at Cassie and she distinctly saw him roll his eyes and Cassie grin as he said, "I guess a day trip couldn't hurt. Let's get you back to the house and see what's happening with the quad. We could leave tomorrow and see what happens. A day of fishing would be right up my alley, and you can just sit there and look pretty."

"That she would," Alex added, laughing as Jess blushed. "You two would have a great time, and if you have time to kill, there's no better place."

CHAPTER 13

What the heck am I doing wasting time with this woman, Kyle thought the next morning as he drove to Jess's house. He'd agreed to Cassie's suggestion to take her fishing, and although he always loved to fish in Gonzaga Bay, he wasn't sure they had enough in common to make it worthwhile and not a torturous exercise in awkward silences.

When he first saw her, he'd thought she was driven, competitive and reckless ... and his opinion hadn't changed. After what he'd gone through with Maggy, he could see the signs and had no interest in even being friends with someone like that. Still, there was something about this girl Jess, something that intrigued him. It was as if she was overtaken by the need to win this race — all races, seemingly — and he wasn't sure why. Away from the quad and the race team, she seemed very uncomfortable, not sure what to do with herself.

He imagined that all of her thoughts led back to the race, and her mission.

He shook the thoughts out of his head as he turned down the dirt road that would take him to her campo, and they were replaced with a fleeting memory crossing his mind of Maggy at the end, in the coma that she would never awaken from. It had been over five years ago, but it seemed as recent as yesterday when he allowed himself to think about it — which he rarely did. It had been too much. He had been too young. And so had she.

As he pulled up to the garage and stopped the car, he pushed the thoughts away. The crew was still working on the bike, the fenders looking a little more like they were fenders rather than accordions. The familiarity of the scene washed through him and he shuddered, a cold chill in his spine. It was just such a scene that was his last of normalcy, and the beginning of the end of him.

"What's the matter, son? You look...not quite right," Mr. McNally said, his eyes narrowing as he looked Kyle over.

"I'm fine, sir. No worries. I'm here to pick up Jess. Taking her fishing. Well, taking her to watch me fish, that is. And only if you still need her out of here," he said, shoving his hands in his pockets and smiling as wide as he could make himself.

"Huh. Well, I hope you're all right, and yes, another

day would be perfect if you could manage it. How's the wrist?"

"Not sure yet. I haven't seen her, but I can check it out in a minute." Kyle turned toward the door, giving a shout for Jess as he knocked on the screen door.

"Come on in," she said from inside, and he let himself in, his eyes adjusting to the cool and dimmer light of the brick house. These houses were his favorite, and they were a welcome relief on the eyes after staring at the desert sand and blue ocean.

As his eyes adjusted to the lower light, he spotted Jess in front of the mirror toward the back of the house, her silhouette framed by the crystal blue water beyond her out the glass doors. Her olive skin and dark curls struck him as beautiful, as if he was seeing her for the first time.

He felt himself smile as she tugged at her hair, trying to get it into a braid. "Don't do that. I like it down," he heard himself say, almost jumping as if it had been said by someone else.

She started and turned to him, her hands dropping to her sides. Her white sundress made it easy to see that she was blushing, and she quickly looked away, setting down the hair tie and grabbing a visor instead. "Well, I guess I could since I don't need to wear a helmet today. Or do I?" she asked, her bright smile turned back toward him.

"No, no helmet today unless you anticipate getting smacked in the head with a fish."

Her laugh filtered through the room, and he was aware that it was the first time he'd heard it. "Well, if I were fishing, that might actually happen. I'm not exactly an expert, but happy to learn. Since there's nothing for me to do here, that is."

"Ah, back to that. Well, sorry to torture you. Feel free to stay if you like." He wondered again why he was torturing her and sacrificing his time. If she really wanted to be working on the bike, it really wasn't his problem.

Her smile faded as soon as the words left his lips. She walked to him quickly, reaching out her hand and touching his arm. "I'm sorry. I didn't mean it like that. You've been so kind to keep me occupied and out of my own way. Really, I didn't mean that."

As their eyes met, he was drawn by the deepness of the brown in hers, and for a moment thought he saw a twinkle of sincerity. Maybe she really could think about something besides racing. Either way, it was just a way to pass the time, and he smiled and said, "No problem. It's not my deal, anyway. But if we're going to do this, we should get going."

"Do I need to pack any food or anything? I can make some sandwiches or something."

"Oh, you cook? That's interesting."

Her laugh again filled the room. "No one on Earth would say that I cook...not well, anyway. I could probably boil an egg if I looked it up on the internet. Cade's a great cook, and we have help at home. I'm really too busy, and not very good at it. But I could probably manage a sandwich that you might find edible. Maybe."

What a big surprise, he thought, looking at this woman who had spent her life doing things other than learning about domestic life. "Alfonsina's restaurant and hotel are right on the bay. We can eat there. If I catch anything decent, they'll cook it for us, too. Complete with the works — tortillas, beans, rice, guacamole." He was rewarded with a smile of relief, and he returned it. "Sounds safer that way," he said as he grabbed her bag and headed for the car.

"Bye, Dad," she said as she waved toward the garage.

"You're not worried that we'll muck it up? Can't believe it," Cade shouted as she continued past.

"I know it's in good hands," Jess said as she moved past the car door that Kyle held open for her, settling in for the next adventure.

The ride down the east coast of the Baja peninsula had been beautiful, the road peaceful and quite empty. She hadn't been down this way in years, and when she had been earlier, she'd noticed only the race track. Today, she was enjoying paying attention to the sights and scenes along the way.

"What's that?" she asked, pointing to a little building in the middle of nowhere with little men made of tubing outside in tiny cars, like cartoon characters.

"You mean Cow Patty's?" he said, looking in the direction she was pointing. "That's a little bar that serves two things...hot dogs and beer."

"Here in Mexico? No tacos? No fish?"

"Nope," he said, smiling. "You're here long enough, and a hot dog can be a pretty welcome sight."

"Somehow, if I were to be away from the U.S. for any length of time, I'm not at all sure that a hot dog would be what I would crave," she said, turning her attention back to the water. "Pizza, maybe."

"Ah, yes, pizza. Have to drive all the way into town for that. Used to be you'd have to go all the way back up north for it. And I just noticed there's a Chinese restaurant in town, too."

"Oh, what is the world coming to?" she said as she leaned forward to look down the cliff toward the water as the road steadily rose before them and they climbed high into the mountains, the drop-off getting very steep.

"Is that the town where they have the hot springs?"

"Puertecitos, yes," he said. "They're great at high tide. Ever been?"

Her eyes clouded for a moment, and she quietly said, "No, I only race, not looking at the scenery much. Guess I'm missing some things."

He hadn't heard her say anything like that before — certainly nothing that didn't involve racing — so he left it alone.

They fell quiet as they peaked the crest of the small mountain range right on the coast, and he pulled over as the view of the islands met them on the other side. The five islands surrounding Gonzaga Bay, Las Encantadas, were beautiful, jutting out sharply from the water and rising high, not far off the coast. At this time of the morning, with the sun rising to the east and warming the water, the sparkles looked like millions of little sparks of steel bouncing off the blue Sea of Cortez.

"The sparkles on the water are — amazing. I've never seen anything like that before." The sight was captivating, and as she leaned over to see them, she realized that she had crossed over into his seat, her hand on his arm, mesmerized by the sight. "It really looks like thousands of little souls playing on the water, doesn't it?" She backed into her own seat as he turned away from the water, his eyes intent on hers. She met his gaze, not looking away.

"What did you say?" He wasn't smiling, but she repeated her comment.

"I said that the sparkles on the water look like millions of little souls dancing. Doesn't it look that way to you?" She smiled as he cocked his head sideways, still staring at her, the corners of his mouth turning up into a grin.

"You may know very little about me, but you do know that I don't like to be laughed at," she said, her own smile spreading on her face. Somehow, it didn't feel like he was laughing at her this time. "Do you know what I mean?"

He turned back toward the water and took a deep breath. "As a matter of fact, I do. I've often thought the same thing, but I've never said it out loud." He cleared his throat, his hand reaching for the key in the ignition.

He gripped the steering wheel, paying attention to the road as he always did. Ever since that day — the day of the accident. He'd never been able to speed again, not on the highway and not on dirt. It just wasn't in him.

And here beside him was somebody who was just the opposite. Completely the opposite. Reckless, with her love of speed. Craving it, risking everything for it. He'd vowed never to have that in his life again.

But here was this same person, the racer, seeing the ocean the way he did, loving Baja and instinctively feeling its warmth and serenity. Seeing the sparkles on the water and thinking about them in the bigger, global context. How could that be? She'd admitted she never looked at anything down here, only had eyes for the race track. Was it just something instinctive in her? Was there more to her than met the eye?

He felt his fingers tighten on the wheel as he ran it all over in his mind, uncomfortable that he was having any thoughts of the sort. He'd been alone and focused only on college and med school since the accident, and that was how he liked it. Nothing and no one could make him risk that amount of pain again. He'd been crushed, hiding behind textbooks, labs and his internship, trying not to feel anything for so long now, he was unwilling to go there.

He breathed deeply, glancing out at the islands and

willing the thoughts away. She was just a girl he'd been tasked to look after. No threat to his comfort, nothing he had to worry about. So what if she liked Baja? Lots of people did. Soon, she'd be back on the quad — and likely falling off again, hurting herself, maybe seriously. And he knew for a fact that that was something he refused to be around for. Nobody was worth that agony again. Nobody.

He loosened his grip and took another deep breath. Besides, she couldn't cook and he really liked to eat. So no concern about a future there. He could forget about it and go back to his comfortable, controlled life.

"What?" she said as he chuckled out loud, amused by the thought of her trying to cook anything at all.

"Nothing, and I promise, I'm not laughing at you," he lied.

"Well, what then?" She tilted her head, her eyebrows raised as she asked the question again very sincerely.

"Really, nothing. Just thinking about food."

"Hm. Not sure I believe you, but I'll let it go this time," she said with a smile. He really did like the way her eyes lit up when she smiled, but he forced his eyes back on the road.

CHAPTER 14

Jess couldn't help but ask about the islands as they passed them on the way to Gonzaga Bay. The five islands ran in a string just off the coast to the east. "Those are called Las Encantadas," Kyle said as he looked past the first, small one.

"Las Encantadas? Does that mean enchanted? My Spanish isn't very good," she said, feeling her face flush again. She'd never cared that she didn't speak Spanish although she'd spent much of her time racing the three annual races on this rugged peninsula. "You know, it's funny how we complain in the U.S. about people not speaking English when they've come from other countries. How many of the Americans here speak Spanish?"

"Precious few," Kyle said, a frown clouding his face. "You'd be surprised. My thought was always if you were going to spend time being hosted by a foreign country and enjoy its benefits, culture and have them share their bounty with you, the least you could do is learn the language. I did it as soon as I could."

"Okay, I'll practice. What's the first island's name?" she said, tugging on the sleeve of his black t-shirt.

"Could be a tricky one. El Huerfanito," he said, raising his eyebrows and looking at her from the corner of his eye. It was the smallest of the five, just a single rock jutting out of the water, not too far off shore, the most separated of all five from the others. "Why is it white?" Jessica asked, staring past Kyle to the unusual sight.

"Um, birds," he said, looking at the sole little island.

"There's so much bird poop that it looks white?" she said, her eyes widening. "Not sure I want to hike there."

"No, me neither. Plenty of other options," he said, as he pointed further out onto the water. "So, first Spanish lesson. What do you think it means? El Huerfanito."

"Hmm. All alone, small...sounds like orphan." Kyle turned to her, his eyes widening equal to his grin.

"You got it. Good one."

Jessica clapped for a moment, then stopped her hands in mid-air. The brace was still on, and she wondered why she was playing this silly game of guess the Spanish words when she should be racing.

As if reading her mind, Kyle stole a glance at her and said, "It's only a little while, Jessica. It's worth the time, the time to heal properly so you don't have to keep doing this over and over again. Taking time out when you clearly don't want to."

"Oh, I want to," she said, embarrassed that she might have hurt his feelings. "I was just thinking of the guys, and getting back in the saddle, so to speak. What's the next one called?"

Kyle ran down the rest of the enchanted islands, explaining that the next one, Isla Miramar, was nicknamed El Muerto, or Dead man.

She looked at him quizzically. "Why the nickname?"

"Turn your head a bit and look," he said, nodding to the island in question.

"Oh, it looks like someone lying on his back with his arms over his chest. Dead," she said, a shiver running up her spine as she saw the likeness in the hills of the island.

The road passed quickly underneath them as he pointed out the rest of the islands. "Isla Lobos is named Wolves' Island, but very few people know it's not named after land wolves, but lobos marinos, sea lions. It's covered with them. And they can be loud, too."

She laughed, imagining a whole island covered with sea lions. "I can't believe I've driven this road countless times for the Baja 1000, either as pit crew or relay driver, and I've never heard all of this." She felt a twinge in her heart as she noticed the beauty and serenity of the water, wondering why she'd never noticed it before.

"Well, I guess you have to be going slow enough to notice," Kyle said.

"Ouch," she said. "That hurt."

"Sorry. Didn't mean to poke. I guess I just think there's more to life than going through the whole thing at high RPM's. Faster isn't always better."

She looked at his hands in the two and ten position on the steering wheel, noticing that his eyes were usually facing right on the road. Did this guy ever have any fun? Faster may not always be better, but she wasn't old and dead yet. A little more excitement was her speed. At least, that's what she'd always thought.

They passed the final two islands, Encantada itself and the largest, Isla San Luis, and headed the last few miles to Gonzaga Bay. They turned west and followed what looked like an air strip, finally reaching the end, almost to the water, where the view opened up into a beautiful bay surround by mountains at the mouth. She drew a quick breath in, startled by the calm waters and rough, desert mountains that plunged in sheer walls of stone into the water. "It's beautiful," she said, her eyes not leaving the water.

"It is, isn't it?" Kyle said, as he turned left, following the single row of houses that covered a spit jutting out into the water.

"Are those airplanes?" she said, sure that the surprise that she felt was clear in her voice.

"Yes," Kyle said, turning his gaze to where she was pointing. "There was a time when most homeowners had to fly down here from San Diego or Calexico. The road we just traveled on for an hour and a half is new. It used to take almost seven hours to drive just from San Felipe. A long time, plus a pretty rough road. Only the hardiest of souls would try to do it on a regular basis."

"So that's what the air strip is for," she said quietly, marveling at this new information. "I had no idea."

"You've been saying that a lot lately." He pulled up in front of what looked to Jessica to be an older, very tropical two story hotel and restaurant. The rustic sign in front read Alfonsina's, and there was actually a parking section for small airplanes, two parked there now.

"Do people just come down for lunch? Fly down?" She craned her neck backwards to look at the airplanes parked outside the restaurant.

"Sure. I've met some really interesting people in the restaurant who've just flown down for Sunday brunch or a margarita," he said as he climbed out of the car. "We can just fish off shore here. I usually catch something. I thought about a boat, but not sure how you'd do in a panga, with your wrist a mess and your foot still sore."

"I'm happy to hold down a beach chair under an umbrella and be the fishing assistant, Cap'n," she said, raising her braced hand to her forehead and hitting it a little too hard. "Ouch," she said, her face scrunched up.

"I hope you're a better fishing assistant than a

subordinate officer. Skip the saluting. It's safer, probably." His laugh started the butterflies in her stomach, and she climbed out of the truck, feeling the warm breeze in her hair. She looked around, wondering if people did this kind of thing often in the middle of the day, on a day right before a race.

***

Jess sipped a cold soda that he'd bought from Alfonsina's while he pounded an umbrella in the sand with the rubber mallet. He'd brought a big umbrella and two chairs and was grateful that it wasn't a particularly windy day as he set up the chairs on the beach of Gonzaga Bay. The restaurant behind them, they had the whole beach to themselves, with just a couple of people paddle boarding further out. Just before the Baja 250, there wouldn't be too many people around as the race route was further inland and he was grateful for the solitude.

"I guess I am pretty much of a loner," he said as she walked up under the umbrella, setting down the beach bag that he'd packed with towels and his tackle box. He'd already asked at the restaurant if they'd cook the fish he caught, so he was hopeful that he'd actually catch something.

He tried to keep his eyes straight ahead as he noticed Jessica settling down under the umbrella in her bathing suit. She'd taken her cover-up off and the suit bore into his eyes as he noticed again just how pretty she was. She wasn't especially tall, but she wasn't petite either. He chuckled to himself, wondering if any girl would appreciate being described as 'not exactly petite', but what he actually thought as he looked at her was that she looked feminine — very feminine in her white bathing suit — but strong and capable at the same time. Except for the brace, which seemed to give her a great deal of aggravation.

"Darn this thing," she said as she struggled to arrange the towel she'd brought. "It really cramps my style, Kyle. When can I take it off?"

He let out a deep sigh, dropping his head in frustration. "I've told you already. You should wear it for at least a month, and shouldn't ride. But especially wear it if you do." He glanced at her out of the corner of his eye, and saw her wrestle her curly hair into a pony-tail before her hands fell to her hips, her chin jutting forward.

"I'm not sure I'll be able to ride with it, and it'll impact how well I can race."

"You know I don't think you should race at all, and not even ride for at least another week," he said as he threw his first cast into the calm waters. "If you do, it will definitely be against doctor's orders."

"Wouldn't be the first time," she said under her breath as she watched him get a strike and reel in his line.

"What did you say?" He watched as the line tightened and he reeled it in slowly, pulling the pole up a little bit each time before he did.

"Nothing. Never mind. What do you have against racing, anyway? You seem adamant about my not doing it."

Kyle frowned as he reeled in his empty line. "Lost it, and it took my hook, too," he said as he sat down in the chair, sipping his beer and reaching in his tackle box for another hook.

"I really need to know what your problem is about racing, Kyle. I don't get it. It's one thing not to want to do it yourself, but another thing entirely to want to stop everybody else from doing it."

He looked down at his hands as he tied a new hook on his line. He glanced at Jessica as she sat next to him, her expression intent. This wasn't a girl he could ignore, and he was positive it wasn't a question he was going to be able to get out of answering.

With a sigh, he said, "I used to ride. Race, too, and I loved it. Somebody I knew was in a racing accident and died."

He heard her sharp intake of breath as her hand flew to her mouth. "Oh, that's awful. I ... I didn't know."

The familiar knot of pain gathered in his heart as he spoke and he wondered if it would ever get easier. "It was a long time ago, but I gave up racing — and riding — altogether and haven't looked back."

"I assume that's why you don't like to speed, and are

such a careful driver?" she asked, resting her hand on his.

The warmth of her touch made his hand tingle, and he stared at her hand over his, surprised. He looked up at her, her eyes soft and her compassionate expression making her look younger, somehow. At that moment, her steely resolve and determination were nowhere in sight.

"Yes. I vowed to go slow, take it safe, and not put myself or anyone else in danger."

"Were you in the accident, too?" she said, reaching into the ice chest for a soda. "Were you hurt?"

Kyle stood, his hook firmly back in place on his line, and cast again into the blue water. The seagulls rose all at once, moving to another spot, the loud flapping of their wings creating ripples on the calm water.

"No, I wasn't. I got to the hospital after the accident, and only got to talk to her once. She was racing, and flipped. Almost just like you did, but she hit her head so hard, even with her helmet on, that she had severe head trauma."

Jess had walked up beside him and looped her arm through his. "She slipped into a coma and never came back out before she died." He felt her shudder as he continued.

"I have wondered since then if there was something I could have done. Something I should have done, and didn't," he said. He quickly started reeling his line in, trying to shake the memory, as Jessica took a step away.

"I am sure there's nothing you could have done. Was she doing something wrong?"

He shook his head slowly as he re-cast his line. "No, it was just a freak accident." He turned to her, resting his hand on her shoulder. "And that's what I've been trying to explain. It's just a dangerous sport, and anything could happen at any time. Especially in a race, where people usually take extra chances. To win."

"Kyle, I don't do that. I'm very good at what I do. I want to win, sure, but I think I do take pretty good care of myself. I'm cautious."

He searched her face as she spoke, and his eyebrows rose as he saw that she truly believed what she'd just said. "Intending to be safe and cautious doesn't make it so. There are a whole lot of variables you're not in charge of," he said, turning back to the water. "As evidenced by the black brace on your wrist."

He felt more than heard her sigh as she turned and walked through the sand back to her chair, sitting down and crossing her arms over her chest. "I guess there's nothing I can say or do to make you understand," she said, pride and determination once again taking over her face.

"No, probably not," he said as his line tugged once again and he started reeling it in.

CHAPTER 15

*J*ess's head whirled all the way home from Gonzaga Bay. The fishing trip had been fun, although she couldn't do much except sit on the shore under the umbrella he'd planted in the sand. The cool water on her feet kept her comfortable as he caught fish after fish and she placed them in the bucket he'd brought, laughing as they squirmed in her hands. She'd dropped a couple, and she and Kyle had raced to catch them.

They'd taken the bucket of fish to Alfonsina's, asking for a few fish tacos each and donating the rest. As a result, they'd gotten a free meal of fish tacos, beans and rice and a margarita thrown in for good measure. They'd laughed as they ate, talking about anything not related to racing or riding, and found they had a fair bit in common. She had thought during their late lunch, with no agenda or timeline, that it had been one of the most fun and relaxing days she'd had. Ever.

It had taken a while for Kyle's mood to lighten once he'd spoken of the accident. As she leaned her head against the window on the way home, she thought how horrible that must have been. She hadn't asked any details about the girl, and she wondered how close they had been, although it was clearly close enough to have changed his life. And left a gaping wound.

They'd fallen quiet on the ride home, and she glanced over at Kyle. That tingling sensation returned in her chest as she looked at him objectively for the first time in a long time. His blond, wavy hair was blowing in the wind from his open window, his green eyes intent on the road. The sight of his strong hands and muscular arms made the tingles sharper as she remembered what his hands had felt like on her the first time they'd met.

She shook her head quickly, hoping those thoughts would go. But they didn't. Every time she saw him, they got stronger and more frequent. After today, and the pain she saw in his eyes as he shared his story, she knew that nothing could ever come of it with racing in between them. She rested her head back on the window, and rested as they sped north, back to the racing team, back to reality.

* * *

"There's my girl," Jess's father said as Kyle brought the car to a stop next to the garage at her house. They'd been silent for the last half hour, and she'd watched the sparkling water rush past her window thinking of all they'd talked about. As she saw her father walk toward them, a familiar steely resolve came over her, and all she wanted to do was to see the quad and hear about how the repairs were going.

"Hi, Dad." She hopped out of the car as he opened the door for her and wrapped his arms around her in a big hug. "How are things going?" she said, almost holding her breath waiting for his response.

Cade poked his head out of the garage as they neared it, a grin from ear to ear. "Hey, Jess, how was it?"

Her palms prickled as she glanced at Kyle, who was looking around her intently. "Yeah, how was it, Jess?" he said, his eyes flickering with laughter. He raised an eyebrow as he waited for her response, a grin on his lips.

"It was fine. Lovely," she said quickly, wanting to leave it behind as quickly as possible. With all that they'd talked about, she was uncomfortable knowing that she reminded him of things he'd rather not think about. She wasn't the girl he'd talked about, and she didn't want to feel like she had any responsibility to be anyone other than who she was.

"The bike's ready to roll, Jess," her father said as he led her into the garage. She saw the familiar blue and white quad, new sponsor decals attached, all buffed and beautiful. "Good as new after a lot of patching and fixing." He rubbed a final smudge off the fender and tossed the rag to Cade, who caught it although he was watching Jessica intently.

Jess smiled at her father and walked to the quad, running her hands over the body work and bending to look at the handiwork below the gas tank.

Mr. McNally returned her smile and squinted at her brace. He turned to Kyle and said, "Still wearing the brace, I see." His face darkened. "She won't be ready to race?"

Kyle took his eyes off of Jessica and met Mr. McNally's gaze. "I've been up front with Jess and told her that I don't believe she should ride at all. But if she does, she'd need to do so with the brace on." He cleared his throat as Jessica stood and turned toward both of them.

"I did hear you say that. I guess I need to talk to the team about it, but I still think you're over-reacting." She bent back down over the quad, checking connections and hoses.

"No, I don't think any of you are listening," Kyle said. "I really don't."

"Dad, what's this hose here? I remember there being a smaller one, but not a red one like this." She tugged at the tube as her father walked over, leaning down and peering at what she was holding.

"Oh, that's just the gas line. It's a different color

because that's the only tubing we could get down here and didn't have any in the van. Somebody used it and didn't replace it, as usual."

She laughed and stood up, turning to answer Kyle, but he was gone. It was just her and her race team in the garage, and she was sorry she hadn't been able to thank him for a great time.

She shook her head, glancing into the distance behind him. As she turned back to the quad, she said, "Cade, what do you think. Are we ready to roll?"

CHAPTER 16

Kyle had opened all the windows of the car to blow his thoughts out of his head. Yeah, he'd left Jessica's in a hurry, but after seeing her turn so quickly back into the racer, he'd just wanted to get out of there. During the last few days, he'd seen a side of her that had just evaporated into thin air when she'd seen the quad and the team, and he wanted no part of it.

He decided to drive up to see Cassie and Alex as he wasn't quite ready to go back home alone yet. He'd be almost all the way to town and could go in to check with Dr. Gomez and see if he needed any help during race weekend.

He rolled up onto the sand, seeing Cassie's red four-wheel drive vehicle over by the entrance to the sanctuary. He saw her, her feet in the sand and her arms wrapped around her knees as she looked out into the gentle waves.

She looked up and smiled as he plopped down beside her, throwing his flip-flops aside and wiggling his toes in the warm sand. She laughed as she patted his knee. "You always did love the feel of the sand between your toes, even when we were little."

"Yeah, and I loved throwing you in the water, too. Especially if you still had your clothes on and not your bathing suit." He reached toward her elbow as she pushed him away, her eyes wide and her hair blowing as she slid further from him.

"Don't you dare," she said. "I'll tell your mom."

His head fell back as he laughed, a deep happiness to his voice that he himself hadn't heard for quite a long time. "Good one. She's not here, and we're grown up. So I just won't do it because I love you. How's that?" he said.

"Thanks. I really appreciate that."

"It's great to see you, Cassie." He picked up a handful of sand and transferred it back and forth between his hands. "What?" he said when he noticed her staring at him.

"I've known you my whole life, Kyle."

"That's certainly stating the obvious," he said, dropping the sand back onto the beach and wiping his hands on his shorts. "Hard not to since we're practically siblings."

She smiled and laid her hand over his knee. "Very

funny, and don't try to brush this aside with humor, like you always do. And don't run away, either."

"Uh-oh. You're implying there's something I need to be prepared to run away from, right?" He stood and walked toward the beach, the cool water washing over his feet as he shaded his eyes, looking for a porpoise.

"You won't see any right now. They're at the far end of the sanctuary, cordoned off. So, I have something to say," she continued, "and I want you to just listen."

He turned as she walked up behind him, his eyes lowered as he waited for what was to come next. Just like his sister, Taylor, Cassie had always been able to read his emotions, tell what he was thinking. He thought he'd just wanted to say hello when he came to visit, but maybe this is what he needed after all. He braced himself to listen to whatever she had to share.

Cassie cleared her throat, and turned to look out over the ocean. "Kyle, when Maggy died, I know you thought your life was over. We were all devastated. You know that."

"Yes, I do. She'd been a part of our lives for so long. I know I didn't have the corner on being devastated. And I don't know what I would have done if you all hadn't been there for me." He pulled his baseball cap on as he cast his gaze down to the sand.

Cassie turned toward him, lifting her hand up to his chin and pulling it up so that she could look into his eyes. "Kyle, there's been nothing after Maggy. Well, college and medical school, yes, but no one after her."

"That's not true. I dated a couple of times," he said, feeling his muscles tighten as he became defensive.

Cassie laughed, tapping her hand on his shoulder. "Two coffee dates in that many years doesn't count. I can certainly appreciate that you wouldn't want to be hurt again like that, but you've got to take your armor off, Kyle. I've seen how you look at this girl, Jessica. Why not give it a chance and see what happens?"

He drew in a sharp breath. Was he really that transparent? He shook his head quickly. A deep sigh left his lips as he turned toward Cassie. Her brown eyes had never left his face, and when he looked at her, he saw sorrow and hope both.

"When Maggy died, you know I vowed never to put myself or anyone else in such a dangerous situation, Cassie. Even though I loved riding as much as she did — our whole family, really — I just couldn't bring myself to do it. Yeah, medical school took up all my time, but even if I'd had all the time in the world, I wouldn't have been able to ride again. I don't even go over the speed limit. Not ever."

As they sat side by side, looking out at the sanctuary, his elbows rested on his knees. His head dropped into his hands, and he felt Cassie's warm touch on his shoulder. She leaned forward and rested her forehead on the top of his head, silent, as he tried to form his thoughts into words. "I like her very much. I really do. She's smart, funny, adventurous, gorgeous, although a little stubborn, maybe. You weren't wrong about that."

Cassie stroked Kyle's hair as she listened. "I suppose it's ironic, then, that she's a racer. What are the odds of that?"

She smiled a little as he turned again to face her. "Maybe she's willing to stop," she said, shrugging her shoulders, the look on her face telling him that even she didn't believe that would be possible.

"Ironic doesn't begin to describe it," he said, his fist hitting his knee. "No, she's driven to win, this race in particular, and I just can't let myself get caught up in it. Yes, it's a shame. But I just can't put myself back into that situation. Not even remotely, Cass."

"I wasn't going to say anything, but I've also noticed how she looks at you. Maybe just wait a while and see what happens?"

Kyle took in a deep breath and stood, offering his hand to Cassie and helping her up. He gathered her up into a hug, lifting her off the ground as she giggled and hugged him back tightly. "You are the most optimistic, ridiculous person I know. Look, there's no decision to be made, nothing to worry about. We're just hanging out, keeping her busy and letting her heal. I promised her dad I'd stick it out, and I will. But don't get your hopes up about anything further. I'm definitely not," he said, as he headed toward his car, waving goodbye as he drove back down the beach.

As he passed by the campos, he thought about what Cassie had said. He'd done his best to ignore her, ignore Jessica, and treat her just as another person he was helping. But in the last few days, he'd come to respect her more, thinking maybe there was something a little more to her, that she understood the dangers of her racing, and that she might agree to be a little less reckless. Maybe even stop racing altogether.

As he passed by Jessica's campo, he turned the wheel sharply and headed up the dune and onto the campo road. He slowed as he neared, intending to stop and see how she was. As he rounded the corner, his foot slammed on the brake and dust plumed around him as the car slid to a stop on the dirt.

There, next to the garage, were Jessica and Cade, all fitted out in their riding gear. As he sat in the car behind them, he watched as Cade took off first, leaving in a plume of dust. His heart skipped a beat as he watched her rev the quad, her leather boots tapping at the gear shift as she took off behind her brother.

He sat and watched until their dust trails faded and they became small specks in the distance. He rested his head for a brief moment on the steering wheel, his knuckles white as he gripped it. He exhaled loudly, realizing he'd been holding his breath. His head shook slowly as he turned the car back toward the beach, and headed toward his own house, Jessica and Cade far behind him.

CHAPTER 17

Jess wiggled her fingers as she gripped the black Velcro. She pulled it tightly around the brace, securing her wrist, remembering her promise to Kyle that she'd leave it on, even if her wrist felt better. She'd tried to get her boots on before now, without the brace, and finally had to admit to herself that it still hurt.

"You ready, Jess?" She heard Cade out in the kitchen and knew he was waiting for her. As she walked toward him, she saw the inquisitive look on his face and turned away.

"What?" she said as she reached for her helmet with her good hand. "I have to try, Cade. You know I do. Don't look at me like that."

"I'm not looking at you like anything. I told you I'd help, and I will. The bike's all ready, and I thought we'd just go around here for a while, see how the wrist holds up. Yes?"

She sat on the kitchen chair and finished buckling her boots, easier now with her brace on. "Sure. Fine. Let's go."

Striding to the door without looking back, she headed for the quad. It'd been days since she'd been on a ride, and she was looking forward to it. Grabbing her hair and trying to wrestle it into a pony tail, she walked into the garage.

"Hey, Jess, you ready?" her father asked as he pushed the quad back out of the garage, turning the handlebars so it was pointing the way she would be heading.

"Dad, I'm fine." She hoped she'd said it loud enough and that they'd quit asking her. Worse than the asking was the way they looked at her. She'd seen him look away when she came in, trying to hide the concern in his eyes. It was almost worse than having them laugh at her, but not much. No pity for me, please, she thought. I'm on it.

She and Cade had agreed that he'd lead and she'd follow, without a crew, just for a little trip around the local desert. They wouldn't be making the trip to the race course until they knew if she could handle herself.

The quad was idling for her, waiting and ready. She climbed on, gingerly testing her fingers and thumb on the throttle, her right hand wrapped in the brace that Kyle had insisted she still wear. She wasn't sure if it would be a hindrance, or cramp her style, but if it did, she wondered if she was willing to take it off and throw it aside, even though she'd promised Kyle she'd leave it on, no matter what.

Cade had hopped on his quad and turned around, his red helmet on and tightened. His quad was bigger than hers, which suited him as he was taller and she saw his head nod, asking if she was ready.

She nodded back and he took off on the course he'd chosen, expecting her to follow. She saw him look back as she took a deep breath and decided she was ready, hitting the throttle and taking off behind him.

SHE FOLLOWED CADE A BIT BEHIND, allowing for enough distance between them so the dust could settle. Her accident had been caused by the inability to see and nothing else, and she didn't want to take that chance again as she gave her wrist a workout.

She gripped the handlebars of the quad tightly as she sped over the dirt roads, standing when she needed to when the bumps got too close together. She felt the familiar rush of speed that she always did when she rushed past the tall saguaro cactus, the pink elephant trees and those deadly cholla cactus. She didn't know much about the vegetation in Baja — she'd never paid attention — but she did know that those were to be avoided.

They'd been riding for over an hour, and the tenderness in her wrist was creeping back. She'd felt great for the past few days, and was disappointed that it was sore at all.

She'd been enjoying the ride, checking out the status of the bike and her muscles, so she and Cade hadn't talked much through their in-helmet radio. Just as she thought she might need a little break, she heard her twin say, "Hey, Jess. How about a break?"

She smiled as she saw him up ahead starting to slow and marveled again at how twins just "knew" what the other was thinking or needing. She and Cade had been close growing up, although they'd had very different personalities, and she was grateful that they had had so much time together as adults, too.

She slowed to a stop beside him, making sure she was downwind and the dust from her quad didn't envelop him. They'd done that to each other on purpose as kids, but now it wasn't quite as amusing — it may have been to her, but she was trying to get through this.

"Power bar?" he said, holding out a nutrition bar that he'd gotten from the saddlebags he carried. He made sure he always had her favorite, taking his job as support crew very seriously. They'd both been wearing Camelback water reservoirs on their backs, drinking from the tubes secured to their helmets, so she didn't feel thirsty.

She unbuckled her helmet with her left hand and

lifted it off, dabbing at the sweat on her forehead with a red handkerchief she kept in the pocket of her riding pants.

"What?" she said, looking over to Cade. He had eaten his power bar and was sitting sideways on his quad, watching her every move.

"So, when are you going to tell me how you really feel?" He rolled up the wrapper of his bar and slid it into the saddlebags, turning away from her for a moment. She heard him sigh deeply as he took a pack of chocolate chip cookies out of his bag and tossed it toward her.

"Aw, my favorite," she said, as she started to open the package, the fingers of her braced hand not cooperating. She tried for a minute longer, eventually opening the package with her teeth and her good hand, looking up as she finally was able to eat a cookie to see her brother staring at her still. His expression was blank as he sat on his quad, his elbows on his knees.

"I will assume, then, that you're still having some trouble with your wrist," he said, his eyebrows rising as he plopped his chin in one of his hands. "You couldn't even open the cookies."

She frowned, her eyes narrowing as she met his gaze. "I'm fine, Cade. It's all fine. The brace is in the way, that's all. Hard to manage with it on."

"Didn't Kyle say you had to wear it, to make sure it wasn't injured more?" he said, reaching for the cookie wrapper and putting it in his bag as she handed it to him.

"Yes, he did, but he's not my boss. Not yours either." Her chin tilted upward, a defiant gesture she'd had since she was a little girl.

"Ah, there's the chin-raise," Cade said, shaking his head slowly. "Jess, do you really know why you're doing this? Have you ever thought about why this is so important to you?"

"You know, I haven't until now. I just haven't. I've done what I thought I should do, one foot after the other, for Dad, for the team. I've just 'done' it. And it's been good for all of us, hasn't it?" she said, her eyes softening as she leaned up against her brother's quad next to him.

Cade was silent for a while as he stared off toward the ocean. He'd always done this when he was thinking, and she'd learned not to interrupt him and his thoughts, that he'd come out with it as soon as he was ready. She followed his gaze, noticing once again the sparkles on the water and wondered why she'd never noticed them before this week.

Cade ran his hand through his hair and rubbed the back of his neck. "Jess, you've been racing since before Mom died. Even as a little girl. Remember when she watched us race? She was so excited."

Jess's memories of her mother were getting dimmer with time, but she'd only been ten when she'd died, at least fifteen years ago. "I do, but it's more just a feeling than a memory. She's been gone longer than she was alive, Cade. I don't remember much.

"Well, I was the same age, but I remember her and Dad being so excited that you were racing and winning even in your age class, and I've often thought maybe that's why you hit it so hard after she died."

She turned to him, her brow furrowing as she tried to understand what he was getting at. "I don't know what you mean."

She felt his hand on her chin as he tilted her face toward his. "This little stubborn chin, and this stubborn girl. You and your racing has held this family together, given us something to rally around, kept us focused. It certainly kept Dad from crumbling when Mom died. But, Jess, we are not your responsibility. You know that. It's not right for you to risk your health — or your happiness for us and the team."

She gasped, her hand on her chest as her heartbeat quickened. She'd never thought about why she wanted to race so badly, she'd just followed along.

"It was good for all of us, right?" she said. "Dad's been into it since the beginning."

"Yes, he has, and he's been very supportive. But I've seen you this past week, with your time off, and I think there are lots of things you might rather do than race. You've actually worn something besides race gear and put on makeup. You're beautiful, by the way, when you look like a girl," he said, laughing and nudging her with his shoulder.

She felt the heat rise in her cheeks at the compliment — she'd always been a tomboy and not had much use for those kinds of things. "Cade—"

"Before you say anything, let me finish. I might lose the nerve, as you've been head of the pack for a long time." He smiled at her and continued. "I've also seen you have fun with a man who seems to really like you. And you can say what you want, but it looks to me as if you like him, too. I've only ever seen you with a random pit crew guy for a short period of time before we travel on. Have you ever thought about having a life? A family?"

She hopped off the quad, pacing back and forth on the dirt road in front of them. The sun had set behind the mountains, and dusk was quickly moving toward twilight, the clouds ablaze in orange and pink.

She stopped and turned toward the clouds, her head tilted upward. She wrapped her arms around herself tightly as the warm wind blew through her hair. "Look at that. Isn't it beautiful," she said, taking her hair out of the pony-tail and shaking it in the breeze.

"What? What's beautiful?" her brother said, looking around.

She laughed and raised her hand, pointing to the glowing clouds. "That, silly."

Cade turned to look at the clouds, turning slowly back to his sister. His eyes narrowed as he watched her. "Who are you? You've never noticed a cloud in your life — that I've noticed, anyway."

She tried to give him her best dirty look as she said, "I do want a life, Cade. I've never known it until now because I've been happy racing. It's all I've known — racing and my family. But this week has been interesting for me. I didn't think anyone would notice, but I guess I should have known you would."

Cade smiled as he hopped off the quad and threw his arm over Jess's shoulder. "I know you've got a big decision to make, and I'm here if you need to talk. I don't want to interfere, and I know there's lots to consider. Have you talked to Dad yet?"

"No, I haven't. Not sure yet what I want to say. I know that things feel different somehow, but not sure how to make it work or what to do."

"Well, if you don't know, you'd better figure it out. And quick. Race is coming up, and you're running out of time."

"Yeah, I know," she said under her breath as she tore herself away from the pinks, yellows and oranges that shifted into the deep blue of the sky as it darkened. She noticed the twinkling light of the first star, and she took in a deep breath, putting her helmet back on and hopping on the quad. "Race you home," she said to her brother as her tires spun and she took off toward the beach.

CHAPTER 18

She pulled the quad into the garage slowly as she returned from her ride with Cade. All the way back, she'd thought about what he'd asked her. Did she really want to do this? Was it worth an injured arm? She wasn't sure of the answer to that, or any of the other questions floating around in her head. Her conversation with Kyle the day before still haunted her. Was there more to life than racing?

"Looks like the bike held up," Cade said with a smile as he took his helmet off and reached out his hand for Jessica's. She tossed it to him and took off her gloves, sliding off the quad and looking at it closely.

"Sure seems that way. I'd say you did a fine job, even if I wasn't here to supervise." She nudged him with her elbow while she massaged her wrist. It had hurt a bit on the way back, but she wasn't sure if it was her wrist or the brace. As she rubbed the feeling back into her fingers, she spotted her father over by the house as he strode toward the garage.

"I heard you guys come back. How'd it go?" He walked immediately to the quad, taking out his flashlight and peering into the engine. "How'd she ride?"

"It was great, Dad. Not a problem at all. Right, Cade?" she said, turning to Cade as he walked into the garage.

"Well, seems like the quad was holding up okay. I didn't see any glitches or notice anything, and Jess says it rode as good as ever." He picked up a gas can, unscrewed the cap to the gas tank and topped off the gas in it. "Looks like it's using fuel the way it should. Not too much."

Mr. McNally set his flashlight on the work bench, leaning up against it and folding his arms over his chest. He turned toward Jessica, who had sat back down on the quad after her brother had finished topping it off. She heard Cade behind her head back outside to his quad, getting it situated as well.

"Well?" her dad asked as she rested, her elbows on her knees. "What about your wrist? Did it hurt? You okay to race?"

She leaned forward, feeling the cool leather covering her knees. The buckles of her riding boots popped as she released them, using her good hand to do it. It was always a nice sensation getting her boots loosened and she silently cursed her braced hand as the fingers slowly came back from numb.

"Dad, why did I start racing when I was little. Do you remember?" she asked, still looking at her boots as her father started to pace.

"What do you mean, why did you start racing? You wanted to. You were hell-bent on racing, and after winning your first one, there was no stopping you."

She smiled at the memory. She remembered her mother on the sidelines, her smile wide, whistling as she cheered her on. One of her clearest memories of her mother, which was strange to her, was that she could whistle very loudly, her fingers between her teeth. Jessica had always listened for it at the end of a race, and sometimes could even hear it over the screaming quad engines.

"The doctor says I shouldn't race, especially without the brace. But the brace is going to slow me down, Dad." She tossed her gloves on the work bench, reaching over to rub her wrist again.

"Jessica, you were born to ride. It's what you do. It's what our family does. What would we do without this?" he said, turning to look out the window at the Sea of Cortez. It was almost dark now, and stars were popping out all over the sky, like sparks of steel, as the sky darkened.

"Is this all there is, Dad? Have you seen the sparkles on the water? Had your toes in the sand?" Her voice was quiet. She came behind her father as he gazed out the window and put her arm through his. "I love you,

Dad, and I've always wanted to keep the family together. But is this the only way?"

He turned to her, his brows furrowed in confusion. "I know I was worried about you, and said some things. But seeing you on that quad today—you're a natural. A winner. This is all you've ever wanted to do. To hell with that doctor. Wear the brace. See if you can win. Don't throw it all away at this point. You win this, you'll be set for life with sponsors. This is what we've — what you've — worked for all this time. You can't quit now. He said you could race with the brace?"

"Well, not exactly. He doesn't want me to race at all. Says it could be bad if I fall," she said, watching her father's face and noticing the flutter in her chest as her heartbeat quickened.

"And just as easily, nothing could happen. You've always been a risk-taker. Don't stop now. Without the brace, you could still win. It's in you, Jess, and the quad is in tip top shape. Do it for the team. Do it for your mother. Do it for Cade."

"Hey, wait a minute. Don't involve me in this," Cade said as he walked back into the garage, pushing his quad to the side of Jess's."

"Not you, too, Cade. I thought you had a better head on your shoulders than that. I don't know what's gotten into the two of you," Mr. McNally said as he slammed the door behind him, storming into the house.

* * *

"I GUESS HE TOLD US," Cade said, shaking his head as the sound of the slamming door reverberated through the garage. "He seems really upset."

"I certainly didn't mean to upset him. Just last week he was worried about my health long term, so I don't know what's changed. I guess I'm just thinking about all of this in kind of a new way."

"I know, Jess. We've just been 'doing' it this way for so long, nobody's stopped and taken any time at all to see if we're really having fun." Cade leaned up against the bench where their father had been moments ago and crossed his arms over his chest. "I didn't mean to eavesdrop, but couldn't help but hear part of that. Mom's been gone for over fifteen years. We can't live for her ... or for Dad, for that matter. I think you owe it to yourself to do some real soul-searching about this. Beyond the risk of hurting yourself, I think it truly has been a lesson that has lots of fall-out. If you hadn't gotten injured, we could have been doing this blindly for another decade. But it sounds like you may be re-thinking."

Jessica sat back down on her quad, her hands running over the cool leather of the seat. She had always loved the smell of a quad — its grease and gas smells wafting in her nostrils and making her feel comforted, like things were familiar. After her mother died, it had become the only comfort she'd known —

racing for her dad and brother, and feeling safe that way. They were all together, as a family. At least as much as they could be with Mom gone.

"What would you do if I stop, Cade? You're a part of this, too." She walked over to him, gently putting her arm through his. Although they were twins, he was much taller, and she rested her head on his shoulder, something she'd done since they were little.

"Jessica McNally, you don't owe me a living. Besides, there aren't too many single girls on the race circuit. And even if there were, we'd be trying to beat them," he said, laughing lightly. "It's not like I'm going to find love on the race courses, either, and moving around so much doesn't exactly say, 'perfect boyfriend' in neon on my forehead."

She squeezed his arm. "I can't believe we've never had this conversation before, Cade. Was it just Dad's dream?"

"Don't go there, Jess. He's just always tried to do what he thought we wanted, for one thing, and what he thought Mom wanted for another. And honestly, I'm not sure he's ever grieved Mom's death. We've kept him pretty busy, between the race circuit and McNally Tires. Maybe that's just how he needed it to be."

"I suppose it's the way we all needed it to be. And maybe we still do. I still want to ride, Cade. There's no reason I can't."

Cade lifted his fist to his mouth and pretended to

cough in it. "Excuse me, yes, there is a reason. Permanent injury? Pain? Doctor's orders?"

Jess's face clouded and she frowned. "He's just a new doctor. In a foreign country. What does he know, anyway?"

Cade's mouth fell open as he stared at his sister, and once he clapped it shut it turned into a big grin.

"Look, you can't fool me. He's a doctor, he's telling you the truth, and I've seen the way you two look at each other. I don't think he's just saying that. If I were a betting man, I'd bet money on the fact that he actually likes you. Beats me why," he said, immediately ducking away from Jessica's hand that struck out at him. "Ha. I knew that was coming."

"That's because you deserved it. He doesn't even notice me. He's just doing his job like Dad asked him to. He had a very bad racing experience once, and has no interest in racing, or even going over fifty-five miles an hour, for goodness sake."

"It might do you some good to slow down a little, Sis. See the sights. Meet a guy. See how you like the normal life." Cade took hold of her shoulders and turned her to face him. "There's nothing wrong with normal."

She reached up and wrapped her arms around his neck, feeling him give her a big hug. "I don't know what I'd do without you, brother."

"I know you're just thinking things through, but I'm here if you need me. And know that I will respect and support whatever decision you make. I do have an opinion, but I'll keep it to myself. You don't need me to tell you what to do," he said, smiling and moving away. "It's late, and I'll see you in the morning. You coming in?"

"Thanks, but I'll be right behind you. Going to sit out for a little bit."

Cade bent and kissed her on the forehead. "Why don't you go out front by the water, and I'll lock up in here. I'll see you inside."

"Thanks, Cade," she said as she waved, heading out the door. The warm, soft breeze caressed her face as she made her way around the house and onto the patio that overlooked the sea. She walked slowly, her mind flooded with memories of when she started racing. She smiled at the memory of that first trophy. The thrill of standing on the winner's podium — with boys to her right and left in second and third place — had been exhilarating. As she thought more about it, she realized that maybe it had been the best one ever, and none after that had ever felt quite so good. And she'd built a life around it, to the exclusion of just about everything. She was beginning to realize what she'd missed.

As she rounded the corner to the patio overlooking the ocean, the smell of sea spray hit her at the same time that she heard the crashing of the waves as they almost reached high tide. The sky was completely dark, but the full moon was beginning to rise, its glow starting to appear on the horizon to the east. As it started to come up, it looked huge, and she stared, almost as if in a trance, at its orange beams shining on the water, reaching out almost as if they were beckoning her to come toward it. It looked like a stairway to the moon, she thought, and felt a shiver run through her as she realized that, although she'd had ample opportunity in the last decade to see this spectacular sight, she'd never noticed.

She sat there for what seemed like an hour, she thought, watching the moon change from orange to yellow to almost white as it reached higher in the sky. She shook her head, realizing she needed to head for bed, and wondered what other spectacular sights she'd been missing.

CHAPTER 19

Two rapid knocks on her bedroom door drug Jess from sleep to consciousness. She'd fallen into bed late after watching the moon rise and her dreamless sleep had been a blessing.

She slowly took in her surroundings and her mouth salivated at the smell of bacon. Cade must be up early, she thought, as she heard the pop of the bacon sizzling in the kitchen, the smell helping her wake up with the added possibility of coffee.

"Jessica, you awake?" Her father slowly opened the door a crack and she smiled, thinking of all the times he'd knocked loudly on her door to wake her up, then seemed surprised that he had.

"I am now, Dad," she said, sitting up as she noticed the lines etched in her father's face. The sight of the dark circles under his eyes made her heart skip, and she managed a weak smile as she waved him in, sitting up and scooting a pillow behind her back as she leaned against the wall.

He smiled weakly at her response, one she'd made what seemed to her at least a million times before. As he sat down at the foot of the bed, she reached out and squeezed his hand. "What's up? You guys are up early," she said as she leaned back against the pillows again.

He stood, walking over to the window that looked out over the ocean. One hand rubbed his wrist as he seemed to be fumbling over his words. Jessica's heart tugged — this wasn't normal behavior from her father, and she wasn't quite sure how to help.

"Didn't sleep much last night, Jess. And when I did, I dreamt of your mother." His hands reached for the windowsill and he unlatched the window, throwing it open to the morning air. He rubbed the back of his neck, and said, "You and Cade made some sense last night, and I just couldn't get it out of my head."

"About what, Dad? Which part?" she asked slowly, not taking her eyes off of him. He'd always been her rock, her go-to guy, and her heart felt heavy as he turned toward her and she saw the pain in his eyes.

"You know, the whole time you guys were growing up, after your mom died, I just wanted everybody to be happy. I know I worked a lot at the tire store, but you guys had Maria to look after you at home, and we had races most every weekend."

She nodded slowly, wondering what had made him so sad suddenly. She hadn't thought of Maria in ages and smiled, remembering the woman who'd come to live with them and look after them. She'd tried to teach Jessica Spanish, but she was never able to keep Jessica from the race track or the garage long enough to do it.

"It was fine, Dad. We were — are happy."

He crossed the room slowly, sitting down with a sigh at the edge of the bed again. 'You know, Jess, I just realized last night, while I couldn't sleep, that we've all just gone ahead at a hundred miles an hour, just keeping busy, just racing. This past week, Cade and I did the same, but I saw you slow down for the first time ever, I think. I always thought you were made for speed, but I'm thinking maybe I was wrong."

"Dad, I'm fine and I intend to win this race," she said, her eyes narrowing as she looked at her father.

His eyes widened and he held his hands up toward her. "Whoa, that's not what I meant. I didn't mean you couldn't do it, just maybe thinking you shouldn't do it."

"Okay, now who's talking crazy, Dad?" She threw the covers off of her and stood up, grabbing some clothes to change into from her pajamas. She tossed several things on the bed before she decided what she wanted to wear — her last clean sundress.

"See, even there you've changed. Before this week, I don't remember ever seeing you look so lovely. Like a girl."

She stopped in mid-stride and looked at him quickly, her face changing quickly into a frown. "Um, thanks a lot."

He shook his head as a grin began to spread across his lips. "Okay, I'm making a mess of this. Let me start over. What I really wanted to say was that I've seen a side to you this week that I've not seen before. Maybe I hadn't been looking, but it's new to me. Your brother kicked me in the head with it earlier, too."

She smiled, wondering what Cade had said to bring about such a change in her father.

"Between talking to him and you last night, dreaming about your mother, and getting it again from him this morning, I just feel like I need to tell you something." She'd sat back down on the bed and was listening intently, her eyes cast down to her hands, which she noticed were clenched together in her lap. He reached for her chin and pulled her face toward his, meeting her eyes with his own.

"Jessica, all I really want is for you to be happy. Yes, we're a team, the three of us and the guys, but your happiness is really what I want most. And if you decide not to race, you have my support. The pit crew will likely be disappointed, but nothing a cold case of beer can't cure." He smiled at her as he squeezed her chin a little and pulled her into a hug. "My beautiful daughter needs to decide what she wants for herself. It's about time, Jessica. Maybe this injury was just your mom's way of getting us to notice."

Jessica turned her head as she saw Cade poke his eyes around the corner of the door, his face filled with interest. She smiled at him, and he let out a sigh, sounding relieved.

"Breakfast is ready, you two," he said, squaring his shoulders and walking into the room.

Doug turned to his son and smiled, extending his hand. Cade took it and pulled him into a hug, slapping his father on the back and holding on a little longer than usual.

"I'll go get washed up and meet you in the kitchen," their dad said, his gravelly voice betraying his emotion as he left the room.

Cade turned to his sister and said, "Went well?"

She nodded slowly. "I guess so. It was strange, but I'm grateful. To him, and to you for your help," she said.

He patted her on the shoulder as he tousled her hair. "Yeah, now comes the hard part. You have to decide what you're going to do."

CHAPTER 20

She was surprised that her wrist felt much better this morning, making her decision even more difficult. She could actually pull on her clothes without wincing and wield a fork like it was an ordinary day. But if she moved it in a certain way, she still felt the piercing tingles in her wrist that hadn't gone away completely.

I need to clear my head and make a decision, she thought as she finished the breakfast dishes and grabbed her flip-flops, wanting to head down to the beach for a few moments. Over breakfast, the three of them had talked over the pros and cons on going ahead with the race, everyone weighing in like the team that they were.

By the end of the discussion, she was as confused as she had been in the beginning, realizing that ultimately the decision was hers and hers alone. As would be the consequences of whatever choice she made.

She knew that she would have a hard time winning if she wore the brace. It had hindered her ability to drive aggressively when she'd ridden with Cade the day before, and it would be a slam dunk for her to win, given the competition this year, without it on. She'd left it at home for her walk, and she circled her wrist and winced as the pain shot up to her elbow. It didn't hurt now with the brace on, but she was certain that she wouldn't win the race with it inhibiting her wrist movement.

As she threw off her shoes and waded into the cool water, she thought of the pain in Kyle's eyes as he recounted the story of Maggy. He'd never told her who she was to him. A friend? A girlfriend? Either way, the memory still gave him a great deal of pain.

She wondered why she even cared. Clearly, with her chosen life and lifestyle, there could never be anything between them. He had been kind to her out of duty, and she understood that he didn't respect her choices. He'd even laughed at her — something no one had done to her before.

She plopped down onto the sand, wriggling in to get more comfortable and leaned back, the warm sun spilling over her. She closed her eyes for what seemed like a second until she suddenly felt a splash of cool water. Sitting bolt upright, she was met with Kyle's wide grin as he splashed her once again.

"Hey, Sleeping Beauty," he said as she laughed, shaking the water out of her brown curls.

"What was that for? I was perfectly content." She laid back down, looking up at the sky as the butterflies came back once again. She clasped her hands over her stomach, hoping that would make them stop.

"Just taking a walk and saw you here," he said, lying down in the sand, the top of his head next to hers. She knew he was behind her, and the butterflies started to really flutter now. At least he couldn't see her as he gazed at the sky, both of them lying on their backs, and she hoped he hadn't noticed the color she could feel creeping into her cheeks. "I noticed you and Cade went out riding yesterday. How was the wrist?"

"Fine," she said, hoping that the curtness of her answer didn't make him think otherwise.

"Ah, okay. So, you going ahead with the race?"

She breathed deeply, letting out a sigh. "I haven't decided, Kyle. I don't think I can win with the brace, and you've made it clear that I shouldn't race without it."

"That sounds like progress. It seems you've been listening to me after all," he said, turning over onto his stomach and perching on his elbows.

"Kyle, who was Maggy? I mean, was she a friend? Of Cassie's?"

She heard him push his arms up in the sand and saw his face over hers, upside down. He looked strange that way, but his eyes still had their depth, their pain piercing her heart.

"She was my fiancée, Jessica. We were going to be married. It was a long time ago now, but she's the only person I've known who made me feel so much. Until now," he said, as he lowered himself over her, his lips meeting hers.

The sensation startled her with its intensity, the butterflies migrating to her throat. Sinking into the heat of his lips, she closed her eyes, feeling her heart warm. Her eyes fluttered open, and she watched as he stood up, walking back up the beach toward his campo. She stared after him, wondering how she could make a decision now, wishing she didn't know how he felt. The weight of the decision she had to make was heavy, and she sat up, drawing her legs to her chest and resting her forehead on her knees as a tear escaped.

CHAPTER 21

Kyle wasn't looking forward to the contingency in town, the time where many of the cars, quads and trucks that were going to be in the race the following day showed off what they had under their hoods. In fact, he hadn't been for years, not since he'd gone with Maggy to see the cars that would drive two hundred and fifty miles at breakneck speed, all trying to win.

Maggy's accident had been the following summer, and the Baja races, along with riding at all, had left his life for good. His friend, Jimmy, had called him on the radio earlier in the morning, though, and asked if he was going.

"I wasn't planning on it," Kyle had told him.

"I haven't been in a long time, and the Tecaté girls are going to be there," Jimmy had responded, his gruff voice carrying a tinge of pleading. "You sure you can't give me a ride?"

"I have no interest in the Tecaté girls, Jimmy," Kyle said, remembering the scantily-clad, beautiful Mexican ladies that came along with one of the race's biggest sponsors. He did have a vague memory of them, dressed in fishnet stockings and very small red dresses, standing in the back of the trophy trucks as they passed by on the malecón.

"What's wrong with you, boy? You're not living, then." Jimmy didn't travel out of Playa Luna much, but it seemed this was one time he really wanted to go.

"Okay. Pick you up in an hour," Kyle said, thinking of the man who'd helped him learn about the desert and the sea, solar systems and scorpions. *It's the least I can do*, he thought, remembering that he really didn't have any other obligations.

He knew Jessica would be there, and wondered if that was the real reason he hadn't wanted to go. "I have to do what's right for me, and for my family," he remembered her saying as she tried to justify the risk she was taking. He'd thought that was a pretty lame excuse for risking your health, risking your life, but when she'd tore off on the quad, even with her brace on, he knew he wasn't going to try to change her mind. If that's how she wanted to be, it wasn't his problem.

He finished cleaning the kitchen, showered, and pulled on some clean shorts and a Playa Luna t-shirt. Campo pride, he thought, laughing at all the different shirts he'd seen around the south campos, each trying to sell the wearer's campo as the best.

"Nice shirt," Jimmy said, grumbling under his breath, which was his version of talking.

Kyle glanced over toward him in the passenger seat as he looked him up and down. "You like it? I can get you one."

"I like my t-shirts. I have three, and that's fine," he said as he glanced in the back seat where his dog, Whiskers, was hanging his head out the window.

Kyle tried to stifle a frown as he thought of Jimmy's meager existence. Kyle checked on him regularly, but his health was failing, his white beard turning even whiter and the non-filter cigarettes he chain-smoked turning his fingers yellow. He'd learned long ago that it was no use trying to change peoples' minds, and that they were going to live the way they wanted to. He'd just have to let that one go, and help as best he could.

As they approached the main stage for the race send-off, the malecón was teeming with people, young and old, racers and spectators. The event was one of San Felipe's most popular, with many of the trophy truck teams letting the young kids sit in the truck — after they'd climbed a ladder to get into them.

"I'm heading down to the beer stand," Jimmy said as he let Whiskers out of the back, clearly experienced in traveling with a dog in big crowds. Whiskers never left Jimmy's side or got into any trouble, and many people in town knew him anyway.

Kyle headed toward the Sea of Cortez with Jimmy, but said, "I'm going to wander for a bit. I'll meet you there." From past experience, he knew that's where Jimmy would park himself, allowing the world to wander past rather than expending the energy to chase it down.

He got down to the main drag, dodging kids with cotton candy and groups of teenagers with too many cell phones, turning left when he got to the street where many of the race vehicles were parked. He set one foot off the curb and jumped back as he heard a loud honk, looking up just in time to see a truck roll past. *Too fast around so many people*, was his first thought, and he felt the butterflies start to flit around his stomach as they did when he was around race cars and lots of people. Now, anyway.

As he stepped foot off the curb once more, looking both ways to make sure he wasn't going to be ambushed again, he crossed the street and paused, leaning against the pole of the traffic signal, and looked down the boulevard.

He didn't have to look far to see the big Team McNally banner, its blue and black coloring standing out in a sea of other colors. The quad was gleaming, and he saw Mr. McNally, Cade and the rest of the pit crew milling around and answering questions of onlookers. He stood stock still, as he realized that someone was going forward riding the quad as it was already registered for the race. Cade, maybe?

He reminded himself that he didn't care who was riding in the race, but he felt his hands tighten around the signal pole, his muscles tensing as he saw Jessica hop down from the back of the support truck, in full riding gear, her brown curls floating down after her and softly surrounding her face. The image seemed incongruent to him, not flowing with her heavy leather boots, blue and black racing jersey and the helmet she held in one hand. As he watched, she reached up to move her hair out of her face. She held her helmet in her left hand, her good one, and as she lifted her hand up to her hair, she looked up and spotted Kyle standing a short distance away. As their eyes met, he continued to stare at her, his emotions racing as he saw she wasn't wearing her brace. She looked at him and looked at her hand, and he saw her eyes widen and heard her say his name.

He broke his gaze, shrugged his shoulders and turned around, walking away to find Jimmy.

He'd thought he didn't care who raced the bike, that it wasn't his business. But now, as his heart thudded in his chest, he wasn't so sure.

CHAPTER 22

"Kyle, wait," he heard from behind, his heart tugging at Jessica's now-familiar voice. His feet almost slipped off the curb as he was pulled backward, his shirt stretched behind him with Jessica's sharp pull. He turned around just in time to see her face change from concern back into steely resolve, her chin raised high and her eyes clear.

"Hello," he said, folding his arms over his chest and taking a step back. "Fancy meeting you here."

Her eyes narrowed as she looked at him, the gold speckles in her deep brown eyes seeming to spark as her hands fell to her hips. If he knew her better, he'd swear she was angry.

"Look, Dr. Lewis, I would like you to know that I am very grateful for all you've done for me and my family this week. It was incredibly kind of you, and I appreciate it very much."

"Kind of you to say so, but it doesn't seem like you've listened to a thing I've said. So, you're going ahead with this, then?"

"Yes. Yes, I am. I've tried to explain what this means to my family ... to me. I can't seem to make you understand. This has been a lifetime in the making, and I have to go ahead," she said quietly. "You said it would be okay if I wore my brace."

He stared at her, his eyes not leaving hers. He could see she was breathing faster now, and he thought he wouldn't be surprised to see steam coming out of her ears. The thought made him smile, and a laugh escaped before he could stop it.

"Don't you dare laugh at me," she said, her voice rising.

"I'm not laughing at you. I said it would be better if you wore your brace, not that it was a good idea for you to race. Besides your wrist being weak, it's just a dangerous thing to do, period." He looked down to the ground, his feet shuffling as he broke her gaze.

"I am not a silly little reckless girl. I am so sorry for what you've gone through. Really, it is heartbreaking. But I am not Maggy. Her accident was awful — what all of you went through is awful."

She took a breath, and reached her hand toward him, stepping onto the curb he was standing on. Her voice had gotten a little louder, and people walking by had stopped, beer in hand, to see what the spectacle was about. He wondered what they did look like as the beautiful racer, in full riding gear, leather boots included, began to poke him in the chest.

"I am not Maggy. Did you hear me? I am not reckless. I know exactly what I'm doing, and can take care of myself." She stopped and took another breath, and he thought maybe she was out of words for a while. *She really is even more beautiful when she's mad*, he thought.

Suddenly, all of the caution that had been so heavy on him for so long seemed to lift. He reached out for her, pulling her to him until his lips were inches from hers and he could smell the sweetness of her breath. He searched her eyes as his heart seemed to thaw, the heat of this girl drawing him to someplace he'd vowed never to go.

He felt her body soften in his arms as she tilted her chin up toward him. "You have to let yourself live again, Kyle, and take risks. Calculated ones, yes. But trust me. I know what I'm doing," she said.

"I guess I hope I know what I'm doing." He bent toward her, his lips searching for hers as he closed his eyes, letting go of all of the memories and visions in his head except for the beautiful one standing right in front of him.

Her arms reached around his neck as she leaned toward him, deepening the kiss, as cheers erupted from the revelers around them. Kyle didn't let her go until he started to hear whistles and applause, his face turning hot in what seemed an instant.

"Si, doctor, bravo," he heard from the people on the

streets. Jessica seemed startled, and she took a step back and tumbled off the curb. He caught her, pulling her to him once again as she regained her composure. His palm rested on her cheek as he pulled her face toward him once more, her deep brown eyes looking at him questioningly.

"Please don't do this," he said softly.

Her hand covered his as she lowered her eyes. When she looked up again, her expression was different. Her face showed no emotion, as if a veil had fallen.

"I have to. I don't know how to explain it any better." She turned quickly, breaking into a jog as she headed back toward her team, her family and the big truck with McNally Racing splashed across the side.

"Then please be careful," he said under his breath, but she was too far away to hear.

"You okay?" Jimmy said as he and Whiskers walked over to where Kyle was still standing on the curb. "That was quite a show." He patted his friend on the shoulder and Whiskers circled them both as they stood watching Jessica head back to her team and her life.

"Was it?" Kyle was still watching Jessica retreat, his shoulders falling as he took in what had just happened.

"Sure was. Looks like you got the girl after all," Jimmy said, nudging Kyle with his elbow."

Kyle turned to Jimmy, his head a little light. "I think it's the opposite, Jimmy. I think I lost the girl ... if I ever had her in the first place. This one just wasn't meant to be, I'm afraid."

"What are you talking about? She's great. Certainly easy on the eyes. And a racer? You used to love to ride growing up. I remember."

"I remember, too, but a lot changed there in the middle. I just don't think I can do it, and worry about her all the time," Kyle said as he ran his hand over the back of his neck.

"She looks pretty capable to me. I checked her out. She wins ninety-nine percent of her races and has never been in an accident. Well, except the one here." Jimmy turned, stopping a vendor and buying a pina colada in a pineapple. "Here, have one of these. I remember they're your favorite."

Kyle sipped the frosty drink, the sweet and sour pineapple matching his mood. "I've been closed up for so long, I'm not sure it's possible to be any other way."

"You are not in charge of the universe, my friend. But if you don't at least allow yourself to be part of it, for better or worse, you're going to be very lonely for a long time."

Kyle swallowed hard and turned to look at Jimmy, his white beard scruffy and hanging halfway to his belt. "What do you know about it? You've been single since I've known you."

"Hey, watch it. There's a lot about me you don't know. I had a life before you came along," Jimmy said, smiling as he turned and walked back toward the car, Whiskers following closely behind.

CHAPTER 23

The adrenaline had kicked in hours before the start of contingency day. Jessica always loved everything about it. It was the most exciting day—people all walking up and down the malecón, checking out the bikes the riders, wishing them good luck and placing bets on who would win. The race wasn't until tomorrow—but this was the show.

Jessica had carefully dressed, making sure that all of her protective gear was in place. Now, as she sat at the staging area with her team, she looked down at the brace that sat in her lap. She felt her brother's eyes on her and she turned, wishing he would tell her what to do.

Her wrist still hurt, and she knew she shouldn't ignore it. This race had been meant to be her big win, her opportunity to solidify her sponsors for the coming years. Her crowning achievement, her moment of glory. Not just for her, but for her team — her dad and Cade as well as the pit crew.

She raised her eyebrows in question to Cade, asking once again for some help. He shook his head slowly, shrugging his shoulders as he smiled and pointed at her, letting her know she was on her own this time.

She stood as her father pointed to his watch, indicating it was time to get to the starting line, and she walked slowly, her head down as the crew pushed her quad to where she would have to commit, and finally decide how she wanted her future to play out.

What future? She thought of Kyle's kisses, knowing that he really couldn't — or wouldn't — be able to accept her racing. She had been eager for his touch, feeling like they'd connected through the time they'd been together and when it happened, her heart had opened in a way she'd not known was possible. And he'd opened her eyes to so many things she'd never noticed before. It was almost as if the world had become new for her, beyond her family, beyond racing.

Even though he could never accept her, she was glad for the time that they'd had. She looked up as she spotted her quad, revved and running, waiting for her to hop on and race. She should be excited, but all she felt was a sense of confusion. If she wore the brace, she probably wouldn't win. If she didn't wear the brace, Kyle would be right and she would be as reckless as all the others, risking injury that could be beyond repair.

As she buckled her helmet under her chin and did a

radio check, she stared down at the brace that was still in her lap.

She looked up at all the people surrounding the racers, the quads, the trucks—big smiles all around with great anticipation for the big race the following day.

Looking over toward the sea, where Kyle had stood moments ago, she realized that he was gone. She knew how he felt, but he was gone. It was left to her now to decide. And she only had one more day to do it.

THE DAY of the race dawned with spectacular grandeur, the oranges and pinks of the clouds as the sun peeked over the water ablaze. As the sun shimmered on the water, Kyle slowly came to consciousness as he awoke. It didn't take long for him to remember his conversation with Jessica the day before, and as he remembered that today was the fateful day, the big race, he sat up slowly and rubbed his eyes with the backs of his hands.

Coffee won't even help this, he thought wryly as he noticed the knot of anxiety in his stomach, wishing it wasn't there. What do I care anyway? If she wants to take that chance, it's on her.

"Kyle, Playa Luna. Kyle, Playa Luna. Come back," he heard over the radio. He walked slowly to it, picking up the handset and responded.

"Kyle here. Go six-eight," he said as they moved

from the hailing channel on the marine radio that was the primary means of communication in the south campos to a quieter one. He laughed at the memory of his first time using the radio, not realizing that it was open and anybody and everybody could listen. He was glad that he'd only asked his mom's friend, Megan, what was for dinner and nothing worse.

"Hey, Kyle, it's Jack. We were supposed to have a doctor at the Shirt Nacho's stop but he bagged out. We'll be watching the race and doing the nachos this year at kilometer twenty-two and were hoping you'd come out. Unofficially, of course. With that many people, it's always good to have a doc on hand. You up for it?"

A wave of dread washed over him, and his hands instantly started to sweat. He hadn't planned on going to the race, actually watching the racers scream by. Hadn't been in years, in fact, since the accident. He wasn't sure he could watch the regular racers, let alone wonder when Jessica would go by.

"Kyle, you there, buddy?"

He cleared his throat and answered, "Yeah, I'm here. I don't know how much help I'll be, but I'll come out for as long as I can."

He could hear the sigh of relief come over the radio as Jack said, "Thanks, man. Free nachos for you, for sure."

"Thanks, Jack," Kyle replied, instantly regretting his decision. The Shirt Nacho guys were doing great work in town, in San Felipe, and this was their primary fundraiser. It had seemed odd to him that people lined up at one of the race markers to get nachos wrapped in a T-shirt, but all the money they made went to buy school supplies, and they delivered them to the school children of San Felipe every year, without fail. It was a good cause, and he thought that's probably why he'd said yes against his better judgment. At least he was trying to 'get back in the world', as Jimmy had mentioned, but did it have to be racing?

He loaded the car with a shade cover, chair and an ice chest and headed out, the sense of dread in his stomach growing as each mile clicked away.

As he pulled up to the tents surrounding one of the mile markers, racers were already coming past, dirt billowing everywhere along the course. He got out of the car and set up his tent after saying hello to Jack, letting them know he was present and accounted for. He had grabbed his medical bag, but hoped he wouldn't need to use it as he sat, glancing around at the eager faces of spectators, all smiling and clapping as the racers came through.

He felt a hand on his shoulder, and turned to see the smiling faces of Cassie and Alex.

"Hey, Kyle, what are you doing here? I never expected to see you at a race, especially this one," Cassie said as she released him from a hug.

Kyle looked down at his feet and shuffled them in the dirt as his hands crossed over his chest. "Jack from the Shirt Nachos asked me to come as a medical assist. I had no intention of coming. None at all," he said, looking past Cassie's shoulder toward the oncoming racers. Cassie turned around and pointed toward the black and blue McNally Racing sign splashed across a support truck.

"Isn't that Jessica's team?" she asked, reaching for Alex's hand.

Alex squinted in the bright sunlight, putting his hand over his eyes to see better. "Sure looks like it," he said, grinning and turning back to Kyle.

"I didn't know if she was going to actually race. It could be her or her brother. I don't see him here," he said, his voice rising over the sound of the various vehicles screaming by.

"Well, mind if we sit with you for a while? The resort is a ghost town with everybody out watching the race, so we thought we'd come out. Maybe we'll get to see her come through," Cassie said, reaching in the back of their Jeep for chairs while Alex grabbed the ice chest.

"Yeah, maybe," Kyle said, plopping into his chair with a thud, his heart beating faster with every racer that drove by.

CHAPTER 24

Her time was good, better than she thought it would be. As she closed in on the pit stop at kilometer twenty-two, she knew she'd have to stop for a minute, at least, to have the crew top off the gas. That had been their plan, and she heard Cade say through their in-helmet radio, "We're here waiting for you. This should be your last stop before the finish line. Be careful. You've got a great time going. So no risks."

"Thanks, Cade," she said as she re-trained her focus on the road ahead of her. She'd had to take a week off, but she'd practiced the course so many times and it was coming back to her with ease.

She rounded the corner of the small dune she was passing, and skidded to a stop. Hopping off the bike to let the crew handle it, she stamped her feet to get the blood flowing. The last eighty miles she hadn't stopped at all, and the pain in her wrist reminded her that maybe she should have.

"Best time ever, Jess. You're on it," Cade said as she lifted her visor and took a sip of the water he'd handed her. "Second place is way behind, best we can tell."

"These single track courses are always tough to see the competition, since you're really racing against the clock," she said. "It's easier if I can see who's right behind me."

"Well, you can see who's right behind you," Cade said, chuckling.

She squinted her eyes at him and wrinkled her nose. "Yes, but it might not be somebody in the quad class. I don't care about the other motorcycles and trucks. I'm not racing against them," she said, taking another swig from the water bottle and finishing it off.

"Cade, have you seen Jess yet?" her father's voice crackled from the radio in Cade's hand.

"Yeah, Dad, she's right here. We're topping off fuel and giving her water."

"Tell her her competition is hot on her heels. She'd better get a move on if she wants to win this thing."

Jessica's eyes went wide. "I thought you said I had a pretty good lead."

Cade shrugged and looked down at her wrist. "Things can change fast, as you know. I see you decided to take the chance and try to win with the brace. I'm glad. Looks like it hurts, though," he said.

She followed his gaze, and her eyebrows shot up as

she noticed she was rubbing her wrist. She hadn't realized she was. "You know it still hurts and I haven't done anything dangerous. Well, except race," she said, managing a weak smile.

Cade leaned toward, taking her by the shoulders. "You know you can stop," he said quietly.

"I know, Cade," she said as she looked over his shoulder and saw Kyle standing, staring at her, his face drawn. "But I won't."

She raised her hand toward Kyle and gave a little wave before she turned and hopped back on the quad, the tugging at her heart something she wanted to leave in the dust behind her. Now wasn't the time to think about Kyle.

The next mile marker was coming up quickly, and she kept her throttle at full speed. "How much of a lead do I have, Cade? How much time do I have to make up?" she said into the radio.

"Looks like you're only about five minutes apart if I'm reading their tracker right."

She shook her head. Five minutes wasn't very much in a four- or five-hour race. *I'm going as fast as I can with this thing on my arm*, she thought, as the nagging pain in her wrist broke her concentration.

The wind whistled through her helmet as her thumb pushed the throttle. Sand crunched beneath her boots as she stood in anticipation of a series of washes that would send her flying if she was going too fast. Dust plumed in front of her, just after the final crest of the washes she was in. Cade hadn't mentioned a crash, but she eased her thumb off the throttle just the same.

As she crested the final wash, she gasped as she turned to avoid a truck being pushed to the side of the road. Her breath quickened as she swerved to the left, the quad on two wheels. Leaning to the left as she started to lose control of the quad, she managed to miss the truck and she bounced from the seat as her two left wheels hit the ground, skidding to a stop.

Her breath came in ragged pants and adrenaline coursed through her veins as she brought her hands to her chest and willed her heart to slow down. She unbuckled her helmet and quickly pulled it off, hanging it on the handle as she tried to catch her breath. She quickly looked back at the truck she'd narrowly missed and one of the crew members waved in apology. "You all right? Sorry, we didn't hear you coming."

She held up a hand slowly, signaling she was all right as she crossed her arms over the headlight and rested her head on her hands.

She'd just been in an accident and flown off the quad not long ago, and had had many narrow misses in her career. As she rested to the side of the course and other racers sped by, she sat up and watched, something she'd not done often. The racers' eyes were so intent, and those who weren't wearing gloves gripped the wheels so hard their knuckles were white.

The sound of Cade calling her from her helmet tore

her from her thoughts, and she quickly placed her helmet back on.

"I'm here, Cade. I'm all right."

"We saw you stop on the GPS. What happened?" he said, worry plain in his voice.

She hesitated, slowly buckling her helmet and pushing it down snugly on her head before she tugged her gloves back on. "Nothing. Just had to stop for a minute. I've probably lost my lead, right?"

"It's still pretty close. If you give it your all, you could still pull it off."

She rubbed her wrist, watching the plumes of dust ahead of her on the course she'd yet to cover. Her eyes were drawn to the right and up, to the biggest saguaro cactus she'd ever seen. It had to be as tall as a three-story building, and she noticed birds flying over and around it, maybe making nests in the tallest of its arms. She felt like she could watch it for hours, and wondered if Kyle had seen it. She fleetingly thought she'd like to show it to him, and that he would love it.

"Jess, you there?" Cade said.

Pulling her attention back to the course, she smiled as she said to her brother, "Yes, I'm here. I really am here."

"Okay, good. Well, if you take off now and ride like the wind, you could still win this."

She started the quad, pulling in the clutch and finding first gear. "I'm going to head out now, Cade, but I'm just going to take my time. There's some cool stuff out here."

She could hear the smile in her brother's voice as he said, "That's my girl. Have a blast. We'll be there when you get back."

CHAPTER 25

"You okay, Kyle? You look a little pale," Cassie said as she walked up behind Kyle. Jessica had come through and waved in their direction, and Kyle had been staring behind her ever since.

Kyle cleared his throat and shook his head. "Yeah. Yeah, I'm fine."

Alex rested his hand on his friend's shoulder. "Mind if I butt in here? I know I haven't been your friend for too long, but I'd like to ask you something."

"What?" Kyle said, turning back toward the race course. He sat back down in his chair, a whoosh of a breath escaping him.

Alex sat down slowly beside him as Cassie's eyes widened. He lifted his eyebrows at her, his hands up. "I have to," he said as Cassie sighed and sat down on the other side of Kyle.

"Alex has a hard time keeping his thoughts to himself when it comes to matters of the heart," she said. She reached over and pried Kyle's hand off of the armrests and smiled. "Relax. It might be painless."

Kyle looked at the white knuckles of his other hand, pulling it back quickly. He leaned back in his chair, his head falling back. "Go ahead. I'm listening."

"We've gotten to know each other pretty well in the past couple of years. At least I think so. And I know all about what happened with Maggy," Alex began softly. "I know that you've kept busy to keep the pain from your heart. And I also know that that can be a very shallow existence." He looked at Cassie, his eyes filled with softness. "I also know that fear of pain is one thing that will keep us not out of pain, but concrete us into it. You can never find joy if you spend all of your time avoiding pain. It consumes you."

Kyle raised a strong arm to wipe at the sweat now trickling into his eye. His chest rose and fell quickly as he looked at Alex. "I know that. What are you getting at?"

Alex stood, and dust billowed from his feet as he moved back and forth, silent. When he spoke, he stopped in front of Kyle, straightened his panama hat and said, "This is a girl who lives life, Kyle. Really lives and goes for what she wants. You enjoy what you're doing, you help people, but playing it safe has its limitations."

"I really don't understand what you're saying, Alex,"

Kyle said, pushing himself slowly out of his chair and squaring his shoulders. Turning his baseball cap backwards, he reached to Cassie and pulled her to her feet.

"Kyle, we love you, and we want you to be happy. You've been alone for such a long time, and seeing you here today has given us hope that maybe, maybe you're ready to move on. Jessica is not Maggy. She's got a good head on her shoulders, and is capable and fun and driven. If you're afraid to get involved with someone because you might get hurt again, you could be alone forever."

"I really do appreciate your help and concern, both of you. But I know what I can and can't do. Yes, she's great, but being with someone who's willing to risk her life on a regular basis is just more than I can handle." He bent over quickly and folded up his chair, throwing it in the back of his car. Picking up his medical bag, he said, "I've spent my adult life vowing to protect lives, not watch them get thrown away."

Cassie slipped her hand into her husband's, tugging at the dolphin necklace she always wore.

"Stop worrying, Cass. I'm fine. And Alex, thanks for your wise counsel," Kyle said, reaching out to shake Alex's hand before he turned to walk away.

"Kyle, I've asked the McNally crew and team over to the resort tonight. We planned a little celebration for them in the restaurant and I'd like you to be there."

The medical bag bounced as he threw it in his car and slid in beside it. Pulling the door shut, he waved out the window as he said, "We'll see," before driving back toward the ocean, leaving the race course behind.

He'd been surprised at what he'd felt when he saw Jessica. His pulse had quickened and he'd actually felt a lump in his throat. While his heart had sunk when he'd seen she was racing, it also swelled with pride as he realized her determination. And when she'd waved and he saw the brace on her wrist, he'd felt a wave of relief like he'd never known before.

Lost in thought, he bounced out of his seat as he crossed a wash and pushed the clutch in, prepared to shift into a lower gear. As he got onto the road, his chest calmed as his hands fell into their familiar position on the steering wheel. He laughed as he saw his hands at ten and two, and quickly moved them, one hand on the wheel as he rested his elbow out the open window, and decided to go home, shower and head over to the resort. What could it hurt?

CHAPTER 26

Kyle had meant to go home and shower, but as he neared his campo, he realized that the racers should be pulling across the finish line soon. He stepped on the accelerator as he passed his camp, not quite sure why he was heading into town, but enjoying the drive. He'd never seen the finish of the race before, and suddenly it appealed to him. Seemed even exciting.

He pulled up to the staging area and parked the car, hopping out and startled by the sights and sounds. Tired, dirty racers were either sitting in chairs with blank stares or cracking beers and toasting each other. Either way, there was a lot of emotion around.

The McNally Racing truck wasn't too far away, and Kyle headed for it, wondering if Jessica had finished yet. Cade was manning the radio as he sat next to the truck, looking over a table spread with maps.

"You're close, Jessica," he said into the radio with a quick wave in Kyle's direction.

Kyle brought his finger to his lips and Kyle smiled and nodded.

"No, Dad's still at the last pit stop with the guys. Just me here. They'll be back in a bit, but you'll beat them."

"Glad I'm going to beat somebody," Jess said over the radio.

"No worries. We won't even know the official results until tomorrow, anyway."

"Maybe, but I know already. But you know what? It was worth it. This has been the most fun racing I've ever done."

Kyle raised his eyebrows as Cade turned to him, telling Jessica, "Okay, bring it home. You'll be here in about ten. Over."

Cade put his hand out to Kyle, shaking it heartily as he said, "Pretty sure she didn't win, but she doesn't seem to care." A grin covered his face and he rubbed the back of his neck. "This is a changed woman. Aside from all that's gone on since the accident, something happened, about halfway through, and she just...changed. Said there were things to see out there."

"Yeah? Not sure what that could be about," Kyle said as he rubbed the stubble on his chin, trying to cover his smile.

Cade pushed his shoulder and smiled. "Oh, come on, you know exactly what. This is all your fault."

"My fault? How's that?"

Cade looked him up and down, his hands on his hips. "Well, if you don't know, I'm not going to tell you. Ask her," he said, turning to head back toward the truck. "She'll be here any minute.

Kyle turned toward the finish line, walking slowly toward it as he thought about what Cade had said. She'd talked only about her wanting to race, that she had to do it. And he'd told her that he couldn't do it, couldn't watch her, but here he was. Couldn't stay away, actually. He finally admitted to himself that he wasn't just curious about the finish of the race. He wanted to see her.

As the thought crossed his mind, he felt the rest of the weight of his guilt, the weight of Maggy, and the weight he'd chosen to carry for all these years lift.

He realized he'd been hard on her, hard on himself as he looked up and saw the blue and black quad and female rider cross the finish line. As he watched her ride over to the racing truck, his stomach knotted as he wondered what he could say to her to make it right.

She threw down her gloves and her helmet and hugged her brother tightly, both all smiles. As she moved back, Cade pointed to where Kyle was standing and Jessica turned quickly, her hand over her eyes against the sun.

He looked at his feet as his face flushed. *Do something, idiot,* he thought as she turned to him, a puzzled look on her face. He took in a deep breath and unclenched his hands, opening his arms wide for her.

She turned to Cade and reached for his hand, squeezing it as they shared a smile. Cade held her by both shoulders, turned her around and gave her a little push toward Kyle. She started walking slowly, her smile widening, and then she quickened her pace before breaking out into a run as she moved toward him, throwing her arms around his neck as he wrapped her in his.

"You okay?" he said quietly in her ear as he nuzzled her hair. "You don't smell all that great."

She pulled back, laughing. "A little dirt won't kill you. And yes, I've never been better," she said as she reached up with both of her hands, cradling his face and pulling him in for the most luscious kiss he'd ever remembered getting. The best because it was from her.

"Ahem," Kyle heard as he sank deeper into the lips of the beautiful woman in his arms.

"Dad?" Jessica said, pulling away quickly from Kyle and taking a step back as she reached for her dad's hand.

Doug McNally smiled and reached for Kyle's hand, giving it a strong shake, before grabbing his daughter into a hug. "I'm so proud of you, darlin'."

"I didn't win, Dad. I just couldn't," she said as he set her back down on her feet.

"Jessica McNally, we talked about this. I told you it

didn't matter. You just needed to do your best. And you did. You would have won if you hadn't had to wear that brace." He pulled at his belt and took his hat off, slapping the dirt off on his thigh.

"Well, to tell you the truth, it wasn't like that. I really think I could have won with the brace on, but something happened."

"I knew it," Cade said as he walked up with four bottles of beer, handing one to his dad, Jessica and Kyle and taking a big swig from his own. "Do tell."

Jessica led Kyle by the hand over to the tent by the race truck. Pulling back the shade cover, she sat down in one of the chairs, setting her beer beside her in the dirt. "I was coming out of a wash and a truck had stalled on the course. I almost hit it and came close to flipping the quad again. They didn't have anybody flagging that the accident was there and I didn't see it."

"What?" her father said, thudding into a chair beside her as he shoved his hat back on his head.

"It was all okay. Nobody was hurt, including me. But I sat there for a minute and just looked around. It was beautiful out there, and I could smell other things besides gas and exhaust fumes for a minute."

"Well, you weren't exactly supposed to be sightseeing, Jess," Doug said as he drained his beer and reached for another from the ice chest.

"I know, Dad. It wasn't quite like that. I just sat there and thought I wanted to do more. See more. Different things, anyway. And I didn't want to worry about not coming back. For some reason, I was worried about that and I never have been before," she said, turning to look at Kyle and reaching for his hand again.

Kyle sat silently, leaning forward and resting his elbows on his knees as Jessica spoke. The golden flecks in her eyes sparkled as she spoke, and he thought again he'd never seen anything so beautiful.

"I didn't think you'd be here, Kyle, but I'm very happy you are. And I have something to say, and you should hear it, too."

"There's more?" Doug said, falling back into his chair as his eyebrows shot up.

"Yes, Dad." Jessica looked down at her hands as they ripped the label off the beer bottle that she was drinking from. "I want to retire from racing."

She looked up, first at her father and then to her brother, who were both staring at her in silence. Kyle's head snapped toward Jessica as he sharply took in a breath. She turned to look at him finally, her face serene and a smile spreading across her lips. "I have things to see. Places to go. A wrist to heal."

"Well, it's about time," Cade said finally, lacing his fingers behind his head and leaning back in her chair. "Right, Dad?"

"If I'd been paying attention better, I wouldn't have been surprised at all. But this week has shown me a different side to things, Jessica, and like I said the other day, I will support whatever decision you make. We don't need to talk about it today, but there's always McNally Tires. You can work there."

Jessica wrinkled her nose. "No offense, Dad, but I don't think that's for me. I don't have any idea what I will do, but I'm pretty positive it's not that."

Her father laughed, and said, "Well, that's probably a good thing. I bet Cade wants to run the shop. Good living, there."

"I sure do, Dad. It'd be an honor, and I think we can have a good time at it. We can still go to the races. Maybe groom somebody else," he said, glancing at Jessica and wiggling his eyebrows up and down as he laughed.

"Maybe," she said, laughing at the thought. "At least maybe you'll have a shot at meeting somebody who's not in a pit crew. A girl even, maybe," she said as she stood up and reached her hand out to Kyle. "I've been invited to a party at a fancy resort. Care to join me?" she said, pulling him to his feet.

"Absolutely. Can't think of anything I'd rather do," Kyle said, pulling her in for another kiss as her father and brother rolled their eyes and left the tent.

CHAPTER 27

"Over here," Alex shouted, his arm held high in the air as he waved Jessica over. His sky blue embroidered shirt set off his Latin coloring, and his white linen pants looked perfect on the billionaire resort owner. Cassie stood by his side, her linen skirt sweeping on the floor and her dolphin necklace shining as her blonde hair swept over her shoulders.

Jessica glanced around the outdoor patio of the resort, the tables all set with colorful linen, the dark, carved mahogany chairs covered with colorful Mexican fabrics. She looked up at the beautiful cover of the patio, held up with intricately carved pillars of dark wood, and could see stars starting to sparkle through the palm fronds covering the beams.

Brown curls flittered around her face as the cool sea breeze swept over the patio, the bright magenta bougainvillea leaves fluttering in the breeze and floating over the tables. Jessica stopped and sighed, thinking she'd never seen such a beautiful sight.

Two hands gripped her shoulders from behind, and she smelled Kyle's musky scent as he nuzzled a kiss on her neck. "What are you waiting for? Let's head over," he said, softly brushing her hair from her face.

She turned to face him, throwing her arms around his neck. "Just taking it all in. It's so beautiful here."

Her cheeks flushed crimson as he stood back and looked her up and down. "It sure is," he said, a sly grin appearing. Her head fell back as she laughed and wondered how everything had changed so quickly, and how she'd gotten so lucky.

Kyle grabbed her hand and pulled her over to where Alex and Cassie sat, at the edge of the patio, pouring champagne into glasses. Cassie stood and grabbed both of Jessica's hands, pulling her closer and kissing her quickly on the cheek. "Look at you. You look gorgeous," she said, holding her hands toward Jessica. "Far cry from the racing outfit."

Jessica hadn't thought she could blush any deeper, but she felt it happening as she said, "I don't often get dressed up. It was fun, and thank you for giving me the opportunity."

"Well, you sure did it right," Alex said, taking her hand and bowing slightly, giving it a light kiss.

Jessica looked quickly at Kyle, sure her face was showing her discomfort, and was met with a smile and a nod of his head. "Yes, you certainly did."

She looked down at her dress she'd bought from a vendor on the way back from the race. It was the first time she'd bought a dress in years, and the first time she remembered ever really caring about what she wore. The dress had been easy to find...light pink linen with elastic straps that fell over her shoulders. She felt pretty in it, and was happy that it had been received as intended.

"Sit here with us," Alex said, pulling out one of the beautiful chairs for his wife as Kyle reached to do the same for Jessica. "The race team will be here in a moment, but we wanted to talk to the two of you first."

Alex reached for a bottle of champagne, filling four glasses and handing them out.

"Cassie and I, as you know, have worked very hard to build a resort here that is light on the land, yet gives people the opportunity to experience the beauty and wonder that is Baja," Alex began. "While we aren't open completely yet, we're gearing up for a full announcement shortly. We've hired a fire captain and a horse trainer, Hanna and Colin whom you've met, preparing for potential disasters and rides on the beach."

"That sounds like a wonderful thing to do, the horse trail riding," Jess said. "There's so much to see, both in the desert and nearer to the ocean."

Alex nodded and continued. "We agree completely. One of the things we've really wanted to do is focus on eco-tourism, reaching out to tourists who want to know about and care for where we live, our ecology.

There are so many things around here to see, from sulfur mines to giant cacti—"

"I saw those," Jess said. "That's what stopped me from winning, that darned cactus," she said, laughing.

"They're pretty amazing, aren't they," Cassie said. "We want to offer quad tours here at the resort to see those things, but with as little environmental impact as possible. We've been looking for someone to design it and to run it. We just haven't found the right person — until now."

Jessica's hand flew to her chest as she looked from Cassie to Alex, who were both staring at her, silent.

"Do you mean me?" she asked, taking in a deep breath.

Alex laughed first. "Yes, we do. We've been talking about it all week, since we first met you. You are a champion racer, an expert mechanic and are interested in all things Baja. We weren't sure at the very beginning, but we are now. We would like you to be the person to run the eco-tours."

Jessica took a deep breath, amazed how much her life could have changed in such a short period of time. The thought of actually having a job where she could explore, meet new people and actually ride her beloved four-wheelers was just too good to be true. And to be near Kyle? Even better. Her brows furrowed suddenly as she wondered how Kyle would feel about that. He would be working here, too, and he should be consulted, if he hadn't been already. She turned to him, trying to read the reaction in his face. "Kyle? Is that all right with you?"

"All right? You've got to be kidding. I think it's a great idea," he said as he lifted his champagne toward her.

She smiled and looked down at her hands. She inhaled, a calm spreading over her heart and her intuition telling her this was exactly the right thing for her. "I don't know what to say. I'd be honored, especially since I quit my job today. I retired from racing as soon as I crossed the finish line."

Cassie and Alex both looked at her, mouths agape. "We thought we'd have to twist your arm. We were—are—willing to offer you quite a substantial salary. What a stroke of luck that you're available," he said, winking at her and raising his champagne glass in her direction.

"Um, I'll still take the substantial salary," Jessica said, her cheeks flushing red.

"I'm sure we can make a suitable arrangement," Alex said as he turned to Kyle, who was looking on, smiling as Jessica made her decision. Kyle squeezed Cassie's hands and fell back into his chair as he rubbed the bridge of his nose.

"Are you okay?" Jessica asked, reaching her arm over his shoulders.

"Yes, I am. I really am. I just had no clue they were going to do that. It seems like a dream come true," he said, standing to hug both Cassie and Jessica.

"What's all this hugging for?" Doug's voice boomed from the door as he, Cade and the crew walked in to join the party.

"Oh, Dad, I have so much to tell you," Jessica said as she grabbed him by the hand and pulled him toward the table.

"Dinner will be served soon," Cassie said. "Clams, enchiladas, barbecued fish — and we'll have plenty of time to talk. Come in and sit down."

Alex stood, clearing his throat and holding his champagne high in the air. "First, I'd like to propose a toast to the winner of the day, Jessica. Congratulations on winning the race, Jess. You were a sight to behold."

"I don't think I won the race," Jessica said. She looked around at her newfound friends and the man that made her heart spin out of control. "But I think I won the best prize after all."

CHAPTER 28

By the time the next race came around, the resort had come alive with racers coming in to stay in droves. The past weeks had flown by, and Kyle and Jess had both settled into their new jobs, taking whatever spare time they had to explore the sea and desert.

It was the week before the Baja 1000, and as the resort was very close to the course this year, and was fully open and operational, Alex had advertised with the race organizer for casitas for their teams to stay in with full use of the quad maintenance facilities that Jessica had planned and built to service their quads for the eco-tours.

It hadn't ever been the case with McNally Racing, but some of the teams could get a little rowdy, and Alex had let them all know that if they wanted to party like that, they'd have to go the short distance into town —

all with a smile and a farewell wave as he closed the bar at the resort early, hoping to prevent too much revelry.

Jess and Kyle sat on the patio, coffee in hand, as they watched the residents in the other rental casitas come alive, slowly but surely, some of then moving pretty slowly and checking on their gear. Some came out wearing boots and helmets already and hopped right in their vehicles, ready for one last pre-run before the big weekend.

"Hey, look at that one," Kyle said to Jess, nodding his head in the direction of the casita next door.

Jess turned and saw a helmeted little girl who looked to be about ten years old. She stared as the girl took her father's hand, walking toward the truck she'd be allowed to ride in today and the truck holding the small quad she'd ride later. "Wow, deja vu," she said softly, watching the father and daughter drive away.

"You sorry you're not racing?" Kyle said, his voice quiet as he searched Jessica's face for any sign of resentment or regret. Not finding any, his breath slowed as she turned to him and smiled.

"No, not even a twinge. I love to ride, but I don't need to race. You cured me of that. I found something better, something that gives me an even bigger rush."

Setting her coffee down, she walked to Kyle and took his cup from his hand. She set it next to hers and sat in his lap, nestling her head against his neck as he wrapped his arms around her.

He was grateful for the gesture, as he'd wondered if

she could be so close to a race weekend, amongst teams, and not be sorry she wasn't joining them. "I was worried that this — that I — wouldn't be enough for you here."

"Are you kidding? I was afraid that I could never compete with Maggy's memory, or make you happy. I've spent my whole life trying to make other people happy that choosing my own path — well, I wasn't sure we'd be on that path together."

"Jessica, I've never met anyone as stubborn, aggravating — "

"Hey, hey. This is supposed to be a nice chat," she said, pushing herself up off his chest, mock horror on her face.

"Or as beautiful, sincere, fun, sneaky..." He laughed as she tugged at his ear, pretending to squeeze.

"Honestly, I'd never met anyone whose heart connected with mine, in spite of our outside differences." He'd never said that out loud, not quite like that, and his heart felt full as she met his gaze, her eyes wide and soft.

"Nor have I," she said. She laced her fingers in his and caressed his cheek. "Our first group of eco-tourists are due today. Everything's ready to go, but I'd like to take a swim first. Care to join me? We can go swim with the sparkles on the waves," she said, standing and reaching out to him. "Come on. It'll be exciting, and I promise, we'll go slow. Just this once."

He laughed as he took her hand, trusting that they

would be safe together, wanting to find the adventure on the other side. With her.

With his warm hand in hers, he followed her toward the water. He smiled as her dark curls bounced and she turned to him, laughing. His heart was full, and he knew that he'd gotten another chance—to love, to be open, to let his heart feel full.

He pulled to a stop, her hand still gripped in his. "Jess, I have something I need to say."

She stopped, too, and turned to him, her eyes questioning.

"What, you don't want to swim? That's not like you," she said, wrapping her arms around his waist and standing on her tiptoes to give him a quick kiss.

"No, that's not it. I love swimming with you." He knew what he needed to say, and that now was the time to say it.

He lifted her chin—the chin that normally jutted up in pride but was now soft in his hand—and lowered his lips to her.

"Before we go in, I need you to know something."

Jessica cocked her head and opened her eyes wide. She set her heels firmly back in the sand, her eyes questioning.

"You've made me live again, breathe again. Not in the scared way I was before, but open, and ready for whatever comes next. And I hope that what comes next is always with you. I love you, Jessica McNally."

Jessica lowered her eyes and her soft, brown curls

swirled around her face. She looked out at the waves sparkling on the water and turned her glistening eyes up to his.

"I love you, too, Kyle. I never knew what I was missing—or that what I was missing most was you."

EPILOGUE

*J*essica walked slowly into the quad garage, looking around in wonder at what she'd created, with carte blanche from Alex and Cassie, in the past year. The twenty quads were all nestled in their bins, gleaming, and she looked at them proudly as she walked to the back. She knew they were all in perfect running order as she'd been the one to ensure it, with her crew of three mechanics, and she knew they ran a great program.

She thought back to the first group of tourists they'd taken out after getting everything situated. Kyle had wanted to tag along, taking a day off from his doctor's duties, and as she'd stood on the step of her quad so she could do a final check of the line behind her, her stomach had fluttered as she spotted him bringing up the rear. It had been his first trip on a quad since the accident, and he'd started out slowly, learning to trust her bit by bit and thawing out in pieces.

She'd waved, blowing him a kiss, and he'd waved back, giving her the thumbs up. She marveled at how much had happened since then, and how they took regular rides in the evenings, spending a lot of time in the giant saguaros, watching the sunset with a picnic in tow.

She pulled at the straps on the storage boxes on the back of the big, 4-wheel drive quads she'd recently bought and gone over with a fine-tooth comb. She put the tents and sleeping bags in one and their food and water supplies on the other, an extra gas can strapped in as well.

Cassie and Alex had brought up the subject of longer eco-tours down the coast of Baja, maybe for seven to ten days at a time, and it hadn't taken much convincing for them to get her to agree. Kyle, on the other hand, had taken a bit more time before he had agreed, but now the time had come. They were leaving tomorrow for a ten-day trip, past the Islas Encantadas and further south, all the way to La Paz.

"Sleeping bags?" Kyle said as he walked into the garage, carrying his fishing pole. "If we're going to camp on the beach, we'll need this for food."

Jess laughed as she tugged the pole out of his hand, nestling it in between the gas can and the plastic food container. "You're going to look like Huckleberry Finn with that sticking out behind you."

"How else am I going to take care of my beautiful fiancée while we're on the road? We have to eat, don't we?"

She smiled, remembering the fish they'd caught in Gonzaga Bay so long ago. "There'll be a few restaurants we can stop at in the smaller towns, but fishing would be good," she said as she walked toward him, wrapping her arms around his waist.

Kyle sighed deeply, resting his chin on her brown curls. "I just can't believe how much has changed. Me, getting on a quad and driving down Baja. I wouldn't do it without you, Jess, and I'm grateful you've brought that back into my life. I hadn't realized I'd missed it so much."

Her cheek warmed on his chest as tears welled up in her eyes. "And I had no idea I was missing so much, so completely. I never would have seen the souls dancing on the waves if it hadn't been for you getting me to slow down."

He lifted her chin up, brushing a stray curl way from her face. "Seems it was no accident, after all, that we were thrown together."

"No, it doesn't seem so," she said as she tossed him his helmet and put hers on. "Ready to ride?"

"Never been more ready," he said as he buckled his helmet, hopped on the quad and followed her down the dirt road and toward the beach.

***

Thank you so much for reading the Vaquita Beach series. This was one of my favorite series—I used to live in a place almost exactly like Playa Luna. Well, exactly. I was happy to be able to share it with you.

You also might like to read about another group and friends and family, who live in Newport Beach. Lifelong friends Jen, Faith and Carrie all are planning to have the best summer of their lives—until it looks like the family beach house may be sold! You can read about it here:

Newport Harbor House

If you'd like to receive an email about my new releases, please join my mailing list.

ABOUT THE AUTHOR

Cindy Nichols writes heartwarming stories interwoven with the bonds of friendship and family that combine what she loves most about women's fiction and romance.

Cindy lives in and loves everything about the southwest, from its deserts and mountains to the sea. She discovered her passion for writing after a twenty-year career in education. When she's not writing, she travels as much as she can with her children who, although adults, still need her no matter what they think.

Feel free to sign up for her list to hear about new releases as soon as they are available as well as extras like early bird discounts. Click here to sign up: Cindy's Email List

Made in the USA
Middletown, DE
05 August 2024

58523304R00113